I0846539

FAERIES AND *Frost*
THE **Mythical Mates** OF *Arcane Cove*

CARLY SPADE

Dedicated to those who've never been bothered by a little nip. 😉

One
Jack

Winter was approaching, and I've always led the charge. The blue magical pulse called me from my throne, the same way it had each passing year. Every winter solstice, the oceans surrounding my kingdom provided portals to other realms. I never knew if there was rhyme or reason to the places, or if the universe chose at random. Their purpose, however, was clear. It allowed me to scour the universe for the one thing I had yet to find after eons of searching—my *mate*. I brought the chill and "nip" in the air as the mortals told the stories, but no one knew of my true mission. After countless places over the course of endless centuries, my hopes of it ever happening dwindled, but I would never stop looking for her.

And when I found her, I'd have a kingdom, a crown, and my soul to offer her in return. Who could ever turn down such a prize? That realization was what kept me going, kept the smirk still playing on my lips as I materialized my clothes into snow drifts. I stood on the shoreline in nothing but the snowflake charm I wore hanging from my neck.

Slipping into the lapping frigid waters was easy for what I was—

the Winter King, the Ice King, the King of Snow. My subjects had given me many names over the ages that I lost count. While the freezing temperatures would kill other beings, it *calmed* my skin, cooling it and forming a crystallized barrier as I swam. It never took long to reach the portal. At first, I feared where it would take me. In my youth, my heart would be racing right about now. Where would I appear? Would this be the time I found her? What would she be like? Now, it was as routine as a morning iced coffee.

Nowadays, I didn't give a shit where I ended up and doubted *this* solstice would be any different than the last. Wherever I'd appear, a good time would follow me. Whatever place I graced with my presence should feel so lucky. My polar bear companion, Nanok, twirled in barrel rolls beside me, his snowy white fur floating around him.

The hazy, glowing lines of the circular portal appearing in the distance, drew my attention. I nudged my chin at Nanok to ensure he trailed close behind me; otherwise, the portal would close without him. The reaction was instantaneous. No sooner had my foot slipped through, followed by Nanok's paw, than we appeared where the portal desired—in more water.

Interesting. This was a first.

Circling a hand, I motioned for Nanok to approach from the farther side. Despite the bear's inability to communicate with me through spoken language, we'd known each other long enough that we didn't need it. I never went anywhere without Nanok, even if I had to hide him from public view. We were a package deal, protecting one another, growing up together since we were cubs.

I floated toward the circle, my fingertips pressing against ice— the entire surface of whatever this was remained frozen over. Balling my hand into a fist, I punched it through the ice with little effort, creating a hole big enough for me to pull myself out of the water.

A grey sky greeted me, a thick blanket of haze and mist hanging over what I could now surmise was a frozen lake. Sputtering water, I hoisted the rest of the way until I stood barefoot on the ice. The droplets still covering my skin froze quickly in the wintry temperatures, my breath turning into snowy wisps. Snowy chunks now clung to my spiky hair and hung from my beard. I wiped them away, making a confident stride over the frozen lake that wouldn't *dare* to crack beneath my bare feet.

It was always too early to tell when I first appeared in unfamiliar territory what form of attire to don. Until I had the chance to survey the land, study its people and customs, I started with something neutral—my grey hooded cloak. It appeared on my shoulders first, rolling out and down toward my feet, my snow blue magic spiraling around it. The hood developed last, and I slipped it over my head, if for anything else but to hide my pointed ears—for now. I was by no means ashamed of them or fearful of beings not accustomed to fae becoming alarmed by them, but it was always best to keep a low profile until I knew what I was working with.

A shoreline appeared through the haze in the distance, a shadowy figure sitting on the ice holding a rod. I pulled the cloak tighter around me, disguising the fact that I was naked under it. When I drew closer, I dipped my head to put my face in shadow. Reaching the mysterious being, I noted how petite they were, guessing they wouldn't have been any taller than my thighs were they standing. They had a flat, broad nose, a bushy, long black beard that hung to the ground, and their ears were half the size of their head. There was a hole cut into the ice, the line on their rod pulling at it, but the being made no move to reel their catch in. Judging by the shocked expression, they'd spotted me *before* the cloak.

"Hej," I said, waiting for the being to respond.

They sat frozen, the rod still bouncing.

"Guten Tag?" I tried next, squinting at the peculiar person now.

Clearing my throat, I adjusted my stance. "Halló."

They still stared at me as if they had never seen a man punch a hole in ice with his bare hand and crawl through it unperturbed.

Considering they didn't understand any other language, I defaulted to English. "What is this place?"

The being gulped and finally blinked, yelping when whatever fish was on the end of their line yanked the rod into the water. "The— the Cove," they answered, voice thick with a Scottish accent.

"Really?" I swiveled my hips. "This doesn't look like a Cove."

"Nae," they responded, shaking their head and making the gold rings braided into their beard jingle. "This place. It's *called* Arcane Cove."

A chill, which had nothing to do with my power, clenched my spine as if the universe tried to gain my attention.

Arcane Cove.

Was this *it?*

"Thanks." Strolling past the miniature being, I paused when they scrambled to their feet.

"Wait, wait. Who the bleedin' Seven Hells are ye?"

Bending forward to bring my hood closer to their face, I said, "I'm quite sure you've heard of me." I bopped their broad nose with a single finger, momentarily freezing it. "I'm Jack *Frost.*"

Two

Sylvie

I'd awoken that morning in my small cottage nestled in the woodlands with nothing but the animals as neighbors. Frost coated the leaves, and a vibrant chill hung in the air. Winter. My favorite season. Snatching a light coat and scarf from the stand near my front door, I threw them on and whisked open the door. The calming scents of winter settling in, combined with the crisp, frigid air circling, had me closing my eyes and sighing contentedly. I walked to the back of my cottage, all but giggling at the cold turning my breath into vapor. Leaves and twigs crunched and snapped beneath my boots before the sound echoed from deeper within the forest canopy. A titanic pair of majestic, icy, ivory antlers appeared first, followed by the friendly, staunch muzzle of my white stag, Fintan.

He lifted his jaw, his pale nose working through the air, already detecting the apples hidden in my pockets. When Fintan moved in front of me, standing at his full height, it put my head near his chest. While white stags and hinds existed in the mortal world, they were rare, and Fintan was much larger than any real stag.

Destiny brought us together, though I was sure of it. We found each other when I'd first moved to Arcane Cove. I'd found him patrolling the area around the cottage I now called home. The house's seclusion and availability gave me all the reassurance I needed to sign the lease.

"Good morning, handsome. Feel that crispness in the air?" I smiled and held out a green apple to him. Fintan nodded his head and gently took the fruit from my palm.

Joining him for breakfast, I removed the other apple and ate, resting my back against a birch tree. Birds squawked and cawed above us as they flew overhead toward a warmer climate. Various biomes were protected from the wards, each harboring different forms of plant life and magical animals. Arcane Cove, in particular, was the only one to experience all distinct four seasons without any worry of things changing due to outside interference.

After finishing my apple, I tossed the core for smaller animals and the soil. Fintan bumped his muzzle under my arm, asking for a hug. I obliged him, wrapping my arms as far as they'd go around his thick neck and stroking his snowy white fur.

Pressing my forehead to his when he lowered his face, I patted his shoulder. "Have an adventure today out there for me, okay? I'll be back this evening."

Fintan snorted before scraping the dirt with his hoof and sprinting into the woods. I watched him until his silhouette blended with the white and brown bark of the birch trees. My bakery was a ten-minute walk from the woods, and by the time I arrived in the plaza, the Cove's citizens were already bustling and harping about the holidays. All beings and monsters celebrated holidays differently here, but no one questioned each other and most definitely didn't judge. It still astonished me how eclectic the Cove was with its inhabitants, and everyone somehow managed to be moderately civil to one another *most* of the time.

The keys clanked in my hand as I unlocked the back door to my bakery: *Muffin Compares to You*. Instinctively, I glamoured my wings away, no sooner had I passed the threshold. I've lived in the Cove for two years now after disguising myself for nearly a century in Norway. There was no need to hide my ears or wings here, given it was a refuge for all beings composed of magic. Humans weren't aware the place existed due to the wards camouflaging it and declining entry for anyone without magic in their veins. No humans to hide from and yet, old habits indeed died hard. I wasn't certain *why* I still felt compelled to disguise myself here.

Scents of butter, bread, and honey still hung heavily in the air from what I'd made yesterday, and the familiarity of it made my chest tighten. My assistant, Aegean, had already left his night shift before sunrise, and, given we were open twenty-four hours, I was here for the day shift.

Glancing at the cupcake clock hanging on the back wall, I scurried to the mixing bowls and ovens waiting for me in the kitchen. Humming to myself, I got to work prepping doughs that'd bake through the day, ensuring that alluring scent would linger, not to mention the tinge of magic I sparked into the flames of the hanging sconces in the shop. It wasn't a coercion spell by any means; otherwise, I'd have far more customers. No, it was more of a beacon for goodwill. I wanted customers to feel happy and carefree in my bakery, even if they decided not to purchase anything. Some people stopped by for a friendly conversation and to bask in the vibes. That was fine with me because I didn't start this business thinking it'd make me rich or set me up for my eternal life. I started it because I wanted to spend every waking day doing what made *me* happy.

After loading several loaves into the stone ovens and various trays of muffins and cupcakes, I wiped the back of my hand over my brow and washed the flour from my hands. Pausing in the mirror to check for flour on my cheeks, I took my hair out of its ponytail, positioning it strategically over my ears and changed into the blue apron I wore out front. Every night before closing, I loaded the fridge with enough treats to stock the display case while waiting for the fresh ones to finish. Grabbing the vanilla cupcakes with teal frosting, I bumped the fridge door closed with my hip and walked into the shop.

Dagnar was already waiting on the sidewalk outside. He rubbed his bare arms and bounced on his heels, shivering. How a burly orc could look so vulnerable from a bit of chilly weather always astonished me. Laughing, I rested the trays on the counter and trotted to the door to open it.

"You know we're always open, Dagnar. Come inside. I wouldn't want you to catch a cold out here or something." I stepped aside, craning my neck back to look at him as he stood almost a foot taller than me.

Dagnar shook his green arms as if it'd been snowing outside and let out a groaning sigh when the warmth of the bakery greeted him. "Thanks, Sylvie. I don't know what it is about winter that these orc bones do *not* agree with. And I wasn't sure if you were open. The sign's not lit up." He pointed a claw at the window.

Tapping the sign and frowning when it didn't light up, I shrugged and moved past him to the display case. "Maybe you should get Sable to knit you a custom sweater." I scribbled myself a note to get the sign repaired.

Sable was the Cove's resident seamstress and a humanoid moth with the prettiest obsidian wings.

"Because they don't come in size extra large times five, you mean?" Dagnar chuckled and all but drooled as he caught sight of the muffin trays.

"No. Because they don't make sweaters for *orcs*, Dagnar." Tilting my head to the side, I noted his demeanor and the way he carried himself today. He was neither happy nor sad, but there was something off about him. "How are you doing this morning?"

"Is that your faerie magic?" Dagnar had bent forward to smell the muffins and remained hinged as he arched a dark green brow at me.

Plucking a blueberry muffin from the tray, because I had a hunch it'd do him wonders, I put it in the microwave behind the counter for a few seconds. "Is *what* my magic?"

"You've always been so good at that. Reading folks. Knowing when something's wrong." Dagnar stood tall now, using his black claws to scratch the back of his neck.

Offering him a reassuring smile, I rested the muffin on a plate, sprinkled a bit of my wintry magic over it to form a light glazed icing, and handed it to him. "Part of it, yes. But mostly intuition."

Dagnar gave me an indignant, crooked smile as he took the pastry from me. "Uh-huh. And I'm sure intuition alone somehow told you precisely what kind of muffin I had a hankering for, hm?"

"Eat up, Dagnar," I replied, grinning brightly. "It'll have you ready to conquer the day. Promise."

Dagnar picked up the muffin, his massive hand making it seem half its actual size. He tossed it around his palm, a wrinkle forming between his eyes. "It's Vila."

The name sounded somewhat familiar, but I couldn't quite place it. "I'm sorry?"

"The reason I seem a bit gloomy. It's because of my girlfriend, Vila." Dagnar's shoulders slumped at this confession. "She went on some trip again. Didn't tell me where. It keeps happening more often, and I'm starting to think she doesn't want to spend as much time with me no more."

That's right. Vila, the succubus. I had a lot of words I wanted to spew on that particular subject, but I tried my hardest not to meddle in affairs of the heart. Not only was it not my jurisdiction, but in a small town like Arcane Cove, sticking your nose where it didn't belong could turn into a bigger problem faster than anywhere else. So, I offered an ear, a sweet treat, and in some cases, a shoulder to cry on instead.

"Sorry to hear that." Frowning, I busied myself with wiping down the already clean counter.

Dagnar nodded, rubbing the two small tusks that protruded over his bottom lip. "Yeah. Anyway, bottoms up, huh?" He consumed the muffin in one easy swallow, letting out a gratified moan once the magic kicked in.

"What do you think?" I found myself rising to the balls of my feet in anticipation. I'd never admit it to anyone, but I thrived on praise. It was one of my favorite doses of dopamine.

Dagnar ate the crumbs from every finger and the plate before answering, "Amazing as usual, Sylvie. Thank you. And you're right. I do feel better." He dug into his pants pocket and rested several *lyyke* coins on the counter. I was about to protest that he'd given me too much, but he held up a claw. "Keep the change. It's the least I could do. And the next time you want an ale, hop over to my cafe and it's on the house."

My cheeks would have turned rosy if such a heat were possible. "Thanks, Dagnar." I bowed my head. "Have a good day and try to stay warm, okay?"

Dagnar barked in laughter and moved toward the door. "Will do. I'll tell ya, you're lucky you don't have to worry about getting cold."

"Yeah," I replied, smiling, but my throat numbed at that. The cold never sent a shiver through my bones like most because I was a *winter* faerie.

Dagnar waved, and I kept the grin frozen until he was out of sight, frowning now and letting my shoulders slump. Was it really luck? Or a curse?

Shaking my head and taking a deep breath to push all negativity out the window, I turned on my heel, ready to busy myself until the next customer, but something made my spine suddenly seize. An icy hot sensation formed behind my eyes, moving through my cheeks and surging between my shoulder blades. The wings itched on my back, begging me to release them. I tried to fight it, but was quickly losing the battle. Running to the kitchen, my snow blue and white wings forced themselves out, flaring wide. My pale blue magic uncontrollably swirled my arms and hands. In the same instance, it all just abruptly *stopped*.

And for the first time in my celestial existence, my stomach *warmed*.

Three

Jack

This place was about as peculiar as it was comforting. I'd been to thousands of realms through countless time periods and had never seen as many different mythical beings and species communing in the same space. Hidden within my grey cloak, I spent several hours studying Arcane Cove's citizens. An orc passed at one point, eyeing me suspiciously but eventually paying no mind before wandering into a café called *The Minty Boar*. There were pixies, gargoyles, demons, and maenads. They'd be hard to spot without a keen sense, but I could smell a shifter's scent on several human-like beings that passed. What they could shift into, however, I couldn't surmise from scent alone.

More beings that looked human at first glance continued to stroll by, and though I could sense the magic thrumming in their veins, some I couldn't tell *what* they were. There'd been a male and female I noted with pointed ears, but they were larger and more prominent than my own—elves and not fae. Not another fae at *all?* It seemed not only odd but unnerving.

At any rate, I'd seen enough to know there was no reason for me to hide, and the attire here appeared average, so I didn't need to stand on ceremony in royal garments. Flicking the cloak off and making it disappear in a shimmering snow flurry, I stood in a pair of dark jeans, boots, and a blue V-neck tee. Rubbing the snowflake charm hanging on a chain around my neck, I paused when a discomforting pang radiated through my skull.

I'd rarely experienced pain, but it was more irritating than it was hurtful. Rubbing the back of my head, I turned the other way, and the feeling subsided.

"Hey there," a female voice said from nearby.

Shaking the disorientation from my brain, I swiveled to face her. She was half my height with ringlets of chestnut hair and two small, tan antlers sticking out from her forehead. "Hey," I answered, scanning her, more for curiosity than perusal. I'd known maenads existed but had never met one. They were usually glued to the hip of the Greek god of wine.

"I don't recognize you. Are you new here?" The female folded her arms, her perky upturned nose discreetly smelling the air between us.

"Just got into town today, actually." I slipped my hands in my pockets, habitually making my muscles tighten—a reflex from the instinct to display myself in front of a potential mate. Though the maenad was attractive, I didn't get any tell-tale signs she was it.

"Oh, yeah? What brings you here?" The female scratched one antler, her hips swiveling as she took more of me in, paying special attention to my beard and wintry full-sleeve tattoo on my right arm.

Breathing in the crisp, clean air, I shrugged. "A change of scenery."

"Well, I'm Aella." She extended her hand.

Taking it, but not shaking, I bent forward to place a chaste kiss on her knuckles. She all but melted into an ironic puddle at my feet. "Jack."

"Jack?" Aella snorted and curled her hand under her chin.

Chuckling, I made ice crystallize in my eyes, my gaze sparkling. "Something wrong with the name Jack?"

"Not at all. It's only been my experience that people use a name like that to hide their *real* name."

Leaning forward again, I blew a light, chilling breath, wafting it against Aella's cheek and making her gasp. "Why does it have to be a disguise? Maybe it's short for something."

The maenad stood with her gloved palm pressed to her face, her mouth still formed in a gasp. "What is it short for?"

It was rare, if ever, I revealed my actual name to anyone, finding it best for the world to know me as they always have, simply—Jack Frost.

A man with long hair and curved black horns cupped his tanned hands over his mouth and shouted, "Aella, we're going to be late, let's go."

"I believe you're being summoned." I jutted my head at who I assumed was the awaiting wine god.

"Yeah, I guess I'll see you around the Cove?"

"Maybe."

Not likely. My time was limited, and she wasn't the female I needed to spend time with if I could only find her because she *was* here.

Once Aella trotted away, I returned to the spot where I'd experienced the skull tremors. They happened again, and, pushing through the discomfort, I kept moving forward, the pangs morphing into an icy-hot current swirling beneath my

14

skin. It pulled at my magic, turning my forearms and hands to ice, snowflakes fluttering my knuckles. It yanked and tethered me until it withered away, leaving me standing in front of a building.

Squinting at the sign displaying the phrase Muffin Compares to You, I got the gut feeling I wasn't going to like this place. Muffins meant food. It meant ovens to make them. And what were ovens? Hot. I *hated* the heat.

All but pressing my nose to one of two large pane windows giving a view of the inside, I eyed shelves of packaged goods, a cupcake clock hanging on the wall, and display cases filled to the brim with all varieties of baked treats and breads. Groaning, I balled my hands into fists against the glass, lightly beating my forehead against it.

This couldn't be happening.

A woman appeared at the counter, looking flustered. Her hair was snowy white, fading to the tips, turning a pale blue. She smoothed her hands down her apron, glancing several times at her back like she'd expected to find something there. When she adjusted her hair, my celestial heart just about stopped beating for a solid five seconds. It was fast, it was subtle, but I'd caught sight of them—pointed ears. *Fae* pointed ears.

This was her. This was my *mate*.

But no, no, this couldn't be right.

Growling, I shimmied out of sight so she wouldn't see me, continuing to watch her. She took several deep breaths and fiddled with her phone as the song *"Build Me Up Buttercup"* played through the shop. She grabbed a duster and waltzed around the shop, dusting shelves and displays and singing along. Pressing my ear to the window, I expected her to be off-key and sound like a screeching cat, but much to my surprise, she sounded—angelic. I rubbed my temple and forced my gaze back to her, squinting through the frosted glass, attempting to get a better look at her face.

She circled closer, and I clung to the building's brick at the side of the window, not caring that I probably looked like a kid staring at a toy window display to anyone passing by. I *needed* answers. Her face finally flashed in my direction, and the ice in my veins momentarily softened—crystalline specks glittered on her cheeks, her smile resplendent, and those radiant violet eyes *bound* my soul.

Fuck.

Closing my eyes, I pushed away from the window and held my face in my hands. I was dreaming. I must've still been in my castle in some form of deep slumber and dreaming about the solstice and searching for my mate. That was the only explanation.

Risking opening one eye, I spied the fae female still waltzing around her shop and dusting like a woodland princess interacting with forest animals.

I was *not* dreaming.

I *had* to figure this out.

And so, taking a deep breath, preparing myself for the warmth that was sure to slap me in the face like a backdraft the moment I opened the door, I walked inside, making the bell hanging above the threshold chime.

Four

Sylvie

When the bell chimed, I couldn't have picked up my phone fast enough, fumbling with it to turn off the music. It was not only a Tuesday, but the slowest part of the day, and I wasn't expecting anyone. An exceptionally tall man strolled in with snowy blonde hair, a matching beard, and the fiercest, glacially blue eyes I'd ever seen. His skin was paler, but the winter-themed full sleeve tattoo wrapped around his right arm stood out more because of it. He wore nothing but a t-shirt and jeans, seemingly unaffected by the chilly temperature. In fact, he pulled at the collar of his shirt as if it were stuffy in here.

My throat turned to sandpaper at the sight of him.

"Hi, hello," I managed to stammer out, clutching the straps of my apron for support.

The man drew nearer, and I had to gulp back a gasp at the sight of his pointed ears. I'd only ever seen elves in the Cove, but his—his were *fae* ears. "It isn't possible," he whispered, his eyes flaring open as if he was confused by something.

Any flutters I'd felt during his entrance had morphed into my own bout of confusion. "I'm sorry? What isn't possible?"

The man squinted one eye at me, shoved his hands in his pockets, and began to peruse the shop. "Is this your establishment?"

Narrowing my eyes at him, I shifted from behind the counter to watch him. "Yes. Are you with the media or something?"

"No. I'm new in town." The man picked up a tin, opened the lid, and sniffed the packaged mints inside, grimacing.

I'd gotten close enough to him now that I could see just how blue his eyes really were. He smelled like snow, vanilla, and pine, and it was turning my brain into tantalizing static. "Oh? What brought you to the Cove?"

He set the tin back on its shelf, not bothering to put the lid on. Crossing his arms, making his arms bulge, he brushed past me. "A woman."

I'd been in the middle of re-attaching the lid when a peculiar zing surged through my stomach, making me drop it instead. "Any, uh, any one in particular?"

His gaze fell to the lid on the floor. I half expected him to pick it up, but instead he pointed and said, "You dropped that," before turning and slowly making his way to the counter.

Letting out an indignant snort, I snatched the lid, secured it, and followed him to the display case. "I'm Sylvie, by the way. Were you also looking to satisfy a sweet tooth, potentially?"

"Not particularly," he mumbled, sweat pooling on his forehead. He wiped it away, his shirt suddenly growing soaked over his chest and down the length of his stomach. "Winter's night, *why* is it so hot in here?"

My thighs pinched together at the more visible view of his pecs and abs from the shirt becoming slightly transparent. I snapped my gaze back to his drenched face. "It's a bakery. There are ovens in the kitchen." I jutted my thumb behind me, a small smile cresting my lips. "Should I be worried about you melting or something?"

His eyebrows shot up, and he rubbed the back of his neck. "I'm not a snowman," he replied haughtily.

Holding my hands up defensively, I tilted my head at him. "I meant no offense, though that was oddly specific."

His gaze suddenly became transfixed on my hair, roaming where my ears were snuggled and hidden beneath it. I fanned my fingers over it to ensure they were still covered, and he paid special attention to my movements. "Do you have a name?"

"Yes," he answered.

If my cheeks were capable of flushing, they would've had my skin turning a deep crimson. "Don't care to tell me what it is?"

The man sucked in a breath and pointed at a tray of vanilla cupcakes with blue frosting. "Can I get one of those?"

"I thought you said you didn't have a sweet tooth?" Grasping the silver tray with my fingertips, I dragged it across the counter, holding it captive between us.

He stepped closer, pressing his palms to the countertop. From this angle, I could tell how truly tall he was—he *towered* over me. "Call it curiosity."

"Sure." Keeping our eyes locked, I slowly pushed the tray toward him, but as he lifted a hand to grab one, I yanked it back. "If you tell me your name, I'll even give it to you for free."

When he reached for it, his arm lingered near a small candle I kept lit at the corner of the counter, and he winced, shifting away from it. "Do names mean that much to you?"

Eyeing the bouncing candle flame for a moment, I shifted my

gaze back to him. "In a small town like Arcane Cove, names are *everything.*"

A devious smirk curved his lips, and he drummed his fingers on the counter. "Jack."

Fireflies danced in my stomach. I gulped down a snowball forming in my throat. "Just Jack?"

Jack's eyes lowered to my throat, bobbing and lazily brought his gaze back to mine. "For now."

Keeping true to my word, I picked up one cupcake and sprinkled my white-and-blue magic over it, swirling dust and sparkles until it settled into the frosting. I held it out to him. "Here you are."

His upper lip curled back, and he circled a finger around the treat. "What did you do? Drug it somehow?"

Gasping, I dropped my hand, the cupcake coming with it. "What? No. It's magic. That's what I do here. It's not just baked goods. I lace them with spells to cure what ails customers."

Jack squinted at me and combed his beard with his fingers. "And you think you know what ails me?"

No one, not a soul, had ever questioned my aptitude for working spells. I flicked my fingernail on my apron strap. "It might not be some cure-all or something, but I promise if you take a bite, it'll make you feel better." Offering the cupcake again, I managed a tiny smile.

Jack stared at it for a solid beat before taking it between two fingers. He didn't eat any, however, and tossed it in his palm with a nod. "I'll save it for a rainy day."

Disappointment deflated me. I wanted to see him take a bite. I desired to see him relax in front of me because I'm the one who made him feel good. And I barely *knew* him.

Clutching my apron straps for dear life, nearly choking myself with them, I shrugged. "Suit yourself."

Jack stepped toward the door, still staring at me like I was the world's most mysterious enigma. "I'll be seeing you, Sylvie."

"Will you?" I asked, scoffing at him.

Jack snickered and bumped his ass against the door. He paused before exiting, saying, "It's Frost, by the way."

A breath hitched in my throat. "Frost? As in *Jack* Frost?"

Jack didn't answer me and winked, a twinkle sparkling in his eye before he left, the door chiming closed behind him.

I stood frozen with my mouth open, staring at the door like I expected him to waltz right back in. Marching, I locked the door and flicked off the open sign, fully prepared to close until my night shift assistant showed up in the evening. I was flustered, irritated, and still somehow wrapped up in how attractive a *stranger* was.

All because Jack Frost had to come around *nipping* at my nose.

Five

Jack

Was this the universe's idea of some cruel joke? It *pulled* me to her like a celestial tether I couldn't have ignored even when my mind tried to protest. I'd never felt anything like it in the centuries I'd been searching. This *had* to be it, but how would it work? Not only did she hide her fae ears, but she worked in an inferno that might as well have been hell itself. Visions of her light, voluminous hair bouncing as she twirled in the shop infiltrated my thoughts. As if that wasn't enough, this beautiful, adorable woman also sang like a damn songbird.

"Fuck," I mumbled under my breath. The cupcake was still in my grasp. I'd wanted to eat it, but at the same time, what if it was good? Like, really good?

"Sounds to me like you could use a drink, boy," a gravelly male voice said.

Searching for the source, I spotted a shorter, older man with bowed legs. He wore a ten-gallon hat, dark blue duster, boots with spurs, and a silver sheriff's star pinned to his blue filigree satin vest. "Oh? How could you tell?"

The man chuckled and pointed a thick, stubby finger at me. "Seein' as I know everyone in this town, I'm gathering you're new."

"I am. Just found this place today. I'm—"

"Nope. Don't give a shit what you are, son. If you're in the Cove, it's because you're supposed to be. Ain't my place to pry." The man shook his head, his thin nostrils flaring from his broad nose. "But I will let you in on a secret." He motioned for me to get closer, scanning around us.

Obliging him, I bent forward, turning my ear to him.

"Finneas' there got the best whiskey in town. But don't go tellin' Dion I said that." The man chuckled and patted my shoulder.

Considering I couldn't be certain who the freezing hells this Dion was, all I could do was offer a grin. I eyed his fingers on my shirt before leaning back. "Secret's safe with me."

"Alright then, newcomer, go on, get. Enjoy your drinks." The man all but shoved me toward the pub, and I adjusted the neckline of my shirt before walking inside.

If you're in the Cove, it's because you're supposed to be.

Sighing, feeling defeated before the day had even started, I sulked once I entered. Warmth immediately crashed over me in waves from every corner, the worst of it wafting from a raging hearth against the opposing wall. Holding my hands up to it, already feeling my insides boiling, I found a table the furthest away from it and plopped into a chair.

A tall minotaur with a gold hoop nose ring, wearing a brown leather apron, prominent tan long horns, and a sprouting of dark brown messy hair atop his head, approached. He rested a grey cocktail napkin on the table in front of me. "What can I get ya?"

"Finneas, I presume?" I snatched the napkin, tearing tiny slits around the edges.

"That's right. Haven't seen you around here. You new?"

After forcing myself to stop fidgeting and resting the napkin back on the table, I leaned back in my chair. "Yeah, but just passing through."

"Oh, yeah? You staying at the inn? Selene makes the best breakfast in town for her guests in the morning," Finneas patted his stomach, the ring through his nostrils lifting as he smiled.

Uncomfortably pulling my collar away from my neck, I adjusted in my seat. "You may find this hard to believe, but I seek less *warming* accommodations."

Finneas stared at me for a beat before shivering and chuckling. "Yikes. Sorry about that. Got a chill up my spine for some reason. I don't know why, considering how toasty it is in here."

The chill had come from yours truly—my subtle attempts at cooling the place off before I sweated through my jeans. "It *is* that time of year."

"Right you are. I love winter." Finneas propped his hands on his hips, drumming his fingers there. "How about a hot toddy? To warm your bones from the frigid temperature?"

"No," I blurted, clearing my throat after gauging his shocked expression. "I was told the whiskey here is the best. Can I get a double on the rocks? Lots and lots of rocks? Maybe extra in a separate glass?"

Finneas gave me a quizzical side eye before nodding. "Sure thing. Be back in a jiff."

Stretching my legs beneath the table, I twirled my iron thumb ring and glanced at the surrounding patrons talking, laughing, and enjoying their beverages. There was a succubus in the lap of

24

her current male victim, a pixie sitting by herself but scrolling on her phone and nursing a steaming cup of something, and a group of male demons chuckling and shoving each other on the shoulders, their spade tails flicking back and forth.

"Here we are," Finneas announced, resting the two tumbler glasses on the table. "That'll be ten lyyke."

Wincing, I shoved my hand in my pocket, making a gold coin from my palace appear before slipping it out. "I'm afraid this is all I have. I wasn't familiar with your currency before arriving." I slapped the coin on the table in front of him.

Finneas' eyes grew as wide as snowballs before taking the coin. "Are you sure? This would mean a pretty damn big tip, friend."

"I'll tell you what, you tell me everything you know about one of the citizens here and we'll call it square." Using my boot, I slid a chair from the table, gesturing toward it.

Finneas let out a hearty chuckle, pressing a hand over his stomach. "Maurice, cover the bar for me for a bit, will ya?"

A man who looked like half of an insect waved a clawed hand at him from the bar.

"So," Finneas started, groaning as he sat down, his knees cracking. "Who are you curious about?"

I took a quick sip of the whiskey and popped an ice cube in my mouth to chew. "The bakery owner. Sylvie?"

"Ah, Sylvie? One of the brightest stars in all the Cove, if you asked me."

Shoving the ice to the corner of my mouth, I raised a brow. "Really?" That came out far too indignant. Lowering my voice, I rolled my shoulders and tried again. "Really?"

"Yeah. I take it you've already met her?" Finneas eyed the uneaten cupcake I'd rested on the table.

Scratching my chin through my beard, I jiggled the glass holding the ice. "Briefly."

"And you haven't taken so much as a bite from that cake?" Finneas scoffed. "Sylvie makes the best sweet treats in the Cove. She laces them with magic and everything."

Inconveniently, my spine straightened with curiosity. "Yes, she mentioned that." Lifting the cupcake, I tilted it left to right. "Do you know what kind of magic?"

"Not sure her kind of magic has a label, but she has this way of reading people. Maybe you're having a cruddy day and could use a pick-me-up, or maybe you're nervous for some big job interview coming up. She twinkles her fingers—" Finneas mimicked the actions over the cupcake. "—and poof. You got a temporary fix in the form of a delectable dessert."

While interesting, it also seemed a bit—intrusive. How could she possibly know what everyone in town wanted? Maybe they wanted those nerves at the interview to keep them humble and not come across as overly confident.

Risking it, I nonchalantly swiped my finger into the cake's icing, bringing it to my lips. "How long has she been here? In the Cove, I mean?"

Finneas sighed and leaned one hand on his knee. "I can't say I keep track of when everyone moved in. I've been here for damn near a century, but I try to keep out of everyone's business *most* of the time."

The points of my ears perked, and when the icing touched my tongue, it seemed to cool my body for a fraction of a second. "You run a place that serves alcohol. Surely it's impossible not to overhear things."

Finneas shrugged and continued to stare down my cupcake like he intended to steal it. "My drinks are for the flavor. Only place magical beings can get a buzz is at Bacchus."

Curling a protective arm around the cupcake and relishing Finneas' frown, I finished my whiskey in one gulp. "Why's that?"

"The owner, Dion, mixes in ambrosia wine. As far as I know, it's the only actual alcohol that affects the likes of us." Finneas thumped a broad, furry hand on his chest.

Smirking, I traced a finger around the empty glass's rim. "Fae have one other source," I whispered, ignoring him when he squinted from not hearing me. "I noticed she has a pointed ear." I pointed to one of my own. "But she seems to hide them?"

Finneas fanned his palms at me like I'd crossed a boundary. Depending on Sylvie's reasons, which, clearly now, there *was* a reason, maybe I had. "Listen, I don't know *everything* about her. Considering how personal that is, sounds like something you should ask her yourself."

Methodically nodding, I tossed several more ice cubes into my mouth. "I appreciate all the information."

"That it? You don't want to know anything else about her?" Finneas blanched, spreading his hooves wide and leaning on his knee.

Taking a full bite of the cupcake now, I audibly sighed as the chilly current glided down my throat and settled into my chest. It made the sweltering fire nearby tolerable. "I think you're right. Anything else I wish to know, I'll ask her."

"Suit yourself." Finneas grunted as he pushed on the table to stand, making the glass of ice vibrate. "See ya around."

"Yeah," I distantly replied, using the tip of my thumb to wipe excess icing from the corner of my mouth. Rising, I tossed back another ice cube and shoved the rest of the cupcake in my mouth before heading for the door.

Nanok would surely be pissed at me for making him wander this long without knowing if we were staying here. I bolted for the forest, a new coolness swirling in my stomach and chest from the ice cube and cupcake magic. It was almost as invigorating as swimming naked in frozen waters. A light snow had begun, collecting on the branches and spreading a thin layer over the grass. I tilted my chin, sniffing the air, but couldn't detect my bear. Calling to my magic, I whistled a unique melody only Nanok could hear. When he responded with his song, I followed it, finding him clawing at what little fish remained in the river.

"Listening to your animal instincts, are you, old friend?" Shoving my hands in my pockets, I leaned on a tree, watching him.

Nanok grunted and jerked excitedly when a fish the size of my foot landed on the bank, and he hurriedly ate it.

"I think we hit a dead end here, Nanok. Normally, I'd be all about sticking around and joining in whatever festivities this place does for the holidays, but Sylvie, she just—" I made a fist with one hand, my jaw tensing. "You know?"

Nanok's jaw rotated as he ate. He stared at me with big, rounded, brown eyes and tilted his head to one side.

"Don't give me that look. You didn't meet her." I pointed at my bear and tossed magic at the branch above me, forming ice down its length. "She hides her ears as if she's ashamed of them. Not to mention she's so overly—" Pausing, I twirled my fingers, searching for the correct word to describe it. "—*nice*. A queen has to have some form of godsdamned backbone."

Nanok's shoulders bounced, a bout of snorting following—his version of a laugh. I narrowed my eyes and kicked a fallen piece of bark with my boot. "Taking her side? Really?"

Nanok finished his fish and marched over to me, using one massive paw to shove my shoulder.

"Hey, what the freezing hells was that for?" Rubbing my shoulder, I pushed him back.

Nanok growled and stomped both paws to the ground, snorting and demanding my attention.

Moaning, I slid a hand down my face and let my arms fall slack at my sides. "Fine. Fine. We'll stay another day, and I'll try talking to her again. Happy? But I'm not promising anything. I'm fairly certain this fae female spits venom when she feels threatened."

Nanok snorted and jostled his shoulders again, plopping his ass on the ground and sticking his back legs out to each side.

A feminine scream sounded from nearby, and the familiar scents of watermelon and sugar plagued my very being. It wasn't just *any* female. That sweet scent was unique to one fae and one fae alone—Sylvie.

Six

Sylvie

My hands flattened to the counter, my shoulders hunched forward, and my breathing *increased*. Reacting to my increasing anxiety, the wings flared out on their own. There had been no fighting the way my body responded to him despite having just met. I'd blame his chiseled good looks, but he had a pompous side to him which had always been a deal-breaker for me.

"It's not possible," I mocked in an exaggerated British accent, even though he hadn't spoken with one. "*What* isn't possible?" Yelling that to the skies, I raised my arms.

The faint scent of something burning hit my nose, and my wings went taut before I sprinted to the back kitchen. Smoke billowed from one oven, and I yelped, grabbing a pair of mittens and hurrying to open the door.

"No, no, no. Please don't be ruined."

No amount of begging could've prepared me for the plume of grey smoke escaping and making me cough. Waving my hand in front of my face, I squinted and waited for the smoke to clear before finally landing my gaze on several bread loaves burnt to a freaking crisp.

Groaning, I grabbed them with my mitten and slammed them on the countertop to cool before tossing them in the garbage. I'd never burnt *anything* in my bakery, which only added fuel to the raging, confusing fire consuming my mind *and* stomach from Jack's little impromptu visit.

"Where did this Frost guy even *come* from?" I whisked off my apron and balled it into a haphazard heap before throwing it on the counter.

While Arcane Cove had its permanent residents, it wasn't unheard of to have others passing through. As many beings called the Cove home, others came here for temporary refuge from the mortal world.

"Sylvie, you're letting some stranger get entirely too far under your skin. Breathe," I encouraged myself, taking a deep breath, wafting my hands toward my face, and letting it out slowly.

After simmering the irritation, I semi-calmly removed the other baked goods from the oven that hadn't crisped into oblivion, packaged them and set them in the fridge. Despite being a winter faerie, the heat hadn't normally bothered me, but an icy chill always felt so much better. *That's* what I needed. I needed some time outdoors to feel the snow between my fingers and hit my cheeks.

Grabbing only my light jacket, I disguised my wings and pulled the coat on. A smile curved my lips as soon as I exited to a wintry light snowfall outside. Flakes collected in my hair and eyelashes, and I stuck my tongue out to let some land there. As I neared the plaza, my gaze focused forward and on the awaiting forest tree line ahead.

Frost had begun to coat the leaves and branches, and I ran my fingers over one. I wondered if Jack had anything to do with it? Did he ice up the forest? Make the snow fall? What did his magic entail?

And *why* did I care?

Snarling, I snapped the wetness from my hand and marched further into the woods, looking for any signs of where my stag may have run off to. If it hadn't been for Fintan's black nose, I might not have spotted him appearing through the branches, munching on a leafy twig with small red berries.

"Hey, handsome," I greeted, my heart filling with delight.

I reached for him, and Fintan met me halfway, allowing me to wrap my arms around his neck and sink against him. Gasping and standing straight from the sudden epiphany I had, I patted Fintan's chest.

"How about a sprint, hm? We haven't done that in ages, and I could really use the wind in my hair."

Fintan's head bobbed up and down, his hoof scraping the snowy ground, and he snorted—stag communication for an emphatic yes. Using one of his antlers as leverage, I hoisted myself to Fintan's back and scratched his neck.

Bunching some of Fintan's fur in my hands, I leaned forward near his ear. "Ready?"

Without preamble, Fintan took off in a fierce gallop, making me screech in surprise. I slid further back toward his ass, but quickly recovered, pressing forward again. The chilly breeze surged over us, and I tossed my hair behind me. My ears were prominently displayed, but here in the woods, here with Fintan, I didn't give a damn.

As we sprinted further into the woods, the branches grew thicker, and the snow fell heavier. It grew so dense that it became more difficult for me to see, and I had to duck at one point or another to avoid being smacked off of Fintan's back by a low-hanging tree limb.

"Fintan, we should probably slow down, I—"

That was the precise moment we came upon a ravine. Fintan reared back, his hooves digging into the ground, but there was so much snow, all he did was slide until we were plummeting over the cliff's edge. I screamed, flaring my wings out, flying and holding onto Fintan for dear life, but he was too big, too heavy. He fell from my grasp, falling and disappearing into the flurry of snow.

"No," I cried out, still hovering with my wings, tears stinging my eyes, my hands flying to my mouth. "Fintan," I yelled, holding an arm above my face to shield from the blizzard forming.

In defeat, I floated to the ground, landing on my knees, and began to sob. "Fintan," I whispered.

Fintan's head suddenly appeared, his brown eyes staring at me, terrified. Wobbling, he walked toward me, clinging to the ground with all four hooves outstretched once he'd made it back to safety.

Leaping to my feet and still crying, I hugged my stag. "Gods, I thought I'd lost you, boy, how did you—"

A person's head appeared, hair snowy blonde and spiky. Jack's face revealed next as he calmly walked up the same way Fintan had. Peering over the edge, I gawked at the icy stairs Jack had conjured, leading down so far that I couldn't tell where they started.

Jack brushed snow from his shoulders, shaking some of it from his hair and beard. "Do you often gallop at full speed in the woods during a blizzard?"

"No, because the Cove doesn't normally get blizzards. Is that your doing?" Pressing my cheek to Fintan's head, I glared at Jack, already blaming him.

Jack smirked and flung his hand back and forth like a maestro, making the snowflakes nearest to him follow the pattern. My gaze couldn't help but follow the motions. It mesmerized me for a spell. "It's more like the winter elements reacting to my presence here—to their *king*."

"King?" I whispered, eyes widening, the declaration jarring me from my haze.

Jack crossed his arms, his biceps tightening against his shirt sleeves. "So, you're a faerie, hm?" He nudged his chin at the wings I'd forgotten were still fluttering at my back.

Zipping my spine straight, my wings flapped erratically before I made them disappear. "You weren't supposed to see them." I hid my ears with my hair and crouched behind Fintan.

"Why not?" Jack leaned to the side to see me.

Yearning to change the subject and fast, I continued to stroke a hand over my stag's fur because it was the only thing grounding me. "You said you're a king. A king of what? Of where?"

"Do you always answer questions with questions without an answer?" Jack lifted his brows, his gaze briefly scanning my hair.

"Your question is far too personal for the short time I've known you. Mine is not. You being a king is assumedly public knowledge, is it not?" I'd felt the compulsion to scratch the tip of my ear as I usually did as a nervous twitch, but held back.

"And there's another question." Jack chuckled and took a few steps closer. "I'm *the* winter king."

"There's only one? I didn't realize such a thing existed, and I live in a magical town filled with the impossible." A tiny smile crested my lips.

"Very true." Jack approached Fintan, opening his palm and letting him come to his hand before petting his muzzle. The sight made my core tingle. Fintan never warmed up to *anyone* that quickly. "You live in a place where orcs and gargoyles roam without care, and yet you still feel the need to hide your petite, pointed *ears*."

If my cheeks were capable of flushing, they'd have turned a billion shades of crimson. Sucking in a breath, I ignored him and stroked Fintan's fur more aggressively. "What—what were you doing in the woods? I don't see many people out here."

"I think you can agree that out here feels quite a lot better than some sweltering sweat box." Jack tilted his head and crouched to catch my gaze. "You didn't—you didn't think I was *following* you, did you?"

Rubbing one of Fintan's velvety ears between my thumb and forefinger, I gave a one-shouldered shrug. "It crossed my mind."

Jack scoffed, inching closer to me. "Don't flatter yourself, faerie. I was already here and heard you screeching." He gestured to Fintan with that tattooed arm, and I gulped down a lump forming in my throat. "You're welcome, by the way, for saving your animal."

Guilt punched at my gut now, and I dropped my gaze to the snow dusting my boots. I'd gotten so into my own head, I'd let my usual thankful demeanor slip away. This was Fintan. My stag could've very well been gone were it not for Jack.

After poking my forefingers together, I combed hair away from my ears, exposing them. "Thank you." The words came out so low that a wind gust carried them away.

"What was that?" Jack asked, cupping a hand near his ear.

Forcing my hands at my sides, I balled them into fists, and my wings flared out on their own. "Thank you. I appreciate you saving Fintan. Not sure what I'd do without him."

Jack shoved a hand into his pocket and scratched the back of his head with the other. His eyes focused on the tips of my ears. "You're welcome. I uh—I know how that feels. Having an animal companion, I mean."

We grew silent for a beat, only the sound of Fintan munching on grass echoing around us.

"Did we just have a—" I gestured between us. "—a moment there?"

Jack shook his head and sidestepped to a tree. "I'd call it more of a momentary truce."

"Momentary? Are you back to hating me?" Crouching, I gathered snow in my palm and sighed from its coolness against my skin.

"Hate is such a strong word. I never said I hated you." Jack's lips curled downward into a surprising frown.

Rising, I continued to play with the snow, switching it from one hand to the other. "You haven't exactly been warm to me."

Jack carved a hand through his hair and walked his fingers up the tree's trunk, giving it glistening, tiny icicles in its path. "I'm the living antithesis of anything warm, Sylvie. I'd say I'm *frustrated* by you."

I paused to watch his magic forming on the tree. It had been so long since I used my own wintry magic, I couldn't help but wonder if mine would look the same. "Frustrated? What have I done to you except being me?"

Jack beat his fist against the bark, his lips parting as if he was about to answer me, but he pursed them instead. "It's complicated."

He was annoyed that I didn't answer his questions about why I was for hiding what I am. Yet, here he was withholding some immense truths. Most people came to the Cove as a form of refuge or to escape the harsh realities of places that aren't as accepting of us. Jack was a king in his realm and clearly came here for someone, but wouldn't tell me who. So, who was she?

"I'm not ashamed, if that's what you think." Flaring my wings wide, causing their glittery glow to intensify, I began to form a snowball.

Jack adjusted his snowflake necklace and sighed, his glacial blue eyes even more cerulean from the falling snow. "You have nothing to prove to me. It either is or it isn't. And I can't come up with a good reason as to why you—"

Before he could finish his sentence, I tossed the snowball at him, hitting him square in the forehead. He sputtered and blinked the flakes on his eyelashes away.

Growling, I turned away from him, my wings folding back as I power-walked through the snow. A plume of snowflakes erupted in front of me, covering my entire head, hair, and shoulders. I gasped and held my arms out at my sides, slowly swiveling to face him, the fury evident on my face from my clenched jaw and ice-splitting glare.

"You started it," Jack countered.

Letting out a high-pitched snarl, I shook my head like a canine. "You're *infuriating*, Jack." Fintan was trotting to my side before I even had to whistle for him. I walked away, fully intending not to turn back around this time.

When no sounds of snow crunching beneath boots came, I let out a peculiar sigh. A part of me was thankful Jack was letting me walk away, but another part of me wanted him to follow me—to, I don't know, to *talk*.

Winter's glow only knew why my body reacted the way it did to Jack. His wintry magic that captivated me whenever he displayed it, perhaps? Or the fact that I've never met another being even a fraction like me?

Hoisting myself to Fintan's back, I leaned fully forward, resting on him. And as my stag carried me to our cottage, I slipped off my jacket to feel more of winter's chill against my skin.

Seven

The winter's magic that sparked in her wings when she'd shown even an ounce of confidence was enough to make my head spin. I'd had myself mostly convinced that there was no future for us, that my search would continue for the foreseeable future. Now ridiculous notions of hope and desperation filled my brain.

With my face shoved into Nanok's fur, I mumbled, "Why can't any of this be easy?"

Nanok huffed, shaking me away, and pounded his paws on the ground.

"I know, I know, I was given an entire kingdom, eternal life, and pristine power. Why would this be handed to me on a silver platter as well, right?" Using Nanok as a leaning post, I propped my shoulder against him, his gigantic breaths lulling me into some semblance of comfort.

Nanok snorted and jostled me.

"Hey, why do you keep doing that? I thought we were pals, and I can't even lean on you?" Adjusting my shirt, I frowned at my bear, a bit insulted by his cold shoulder routine.

Nanok bristled his fur, and with a flick of his short, puffy tail, he turned away and strolled into the woods. He picked a hell of a moment to want some "alone time"—the bastard.

"Fine," I shouted. "I see how it is. Maybe I can find a cute little arctic fox to be my companion. One I could carry in my pocket."

Nanok, unimpressed, huffed and disappeared out of sight.

"Great. Just what I need, some quality alone time with my erratic thoughts." Wiggling my fingers at the ground, I conjured an icy path, gliding on it like a surfer on a wave. It'd been so long since I'd done it that the fear of slipping and falling on my ass was an afterthought. At least Sylvie wouldn't be around to witness it. Although it'd probably make her laugh, and that *smile* of hers?

Tensing, I dug my heels into the ice, sending it in a spiraling spray. Why was the idea of making her laugh, even at the expense of my own ego, suddenly so damn intoxicating?

"Fucking yeti's frozen balls," I roared, pinching the bridge of my nose from the brain freeze carving through my skull.

My magic lashed out at that, sending a pulsing wave of icy blue ringlets through the surrounding forests. It vibrated the trees, made birds fly away in alarm, and squirrels scurried to their nests.

A monstrous groan emanated from a frozen batch of rocks, a giant icy head protruding from them, followed by a torso, arms, and legs.

"Great work, Jack. Now you're randomly summoning frost giants. Real responsible, your *highness*," I mumbled.

The giant stretched his arms, his height challenging the birch trees surrounding us, and he parted one tree's branches to peer down at me. He had no real eyes, only two rounded areas carved into his spiky skull, the ice above them shifting as if he were raising an eyebrow. "King Jakzair, why have you summoned me to this—place?"

My given name sent a chill down my spine. No one had called me that in centuries, but the frost giant had probably been slumbering for that long until I went ahead and woke his ass up.

"Apologies, it was, well, an accident." The unease in my tone had me rubbing the back of my neck.

I blamed *her*. I entirely blamed her for my stuttering incompetence.

"An accident?" The giant repeated, mirth lacing his tone, before he let the branches snap back into place. "And why are we not in Norway? What is this place? The magic here—is enchanting."

"They call it Arcane Cove. I couldn't be certain, but it seems that no humans are allowed in. Sorcerer wards are protecting it, I imagine." Panning my gaze to the skies, I focused on the clouds. They were subtle, but if one stared long enough, they'd catch the brief flashes of purple magic.

"That would explain why I feel so spry," the giant added, a throaty, deep chuckle vibrating from his chest. He groaned as he sank toward the ground, sitting on the same pile of rocks he had emerged from.

"Again, I apologize. I know how long it'll take for you to put yourself back into hibernation. But there are no wars to fight here." Spiraling my hand, I created a makeshift ice throne and plopped onto it, letting one leg dangle over an armrest.

The giant curled his long, spiky fingers around what would be his knees and tilted his head upward, letting the snow coat his face. "This isn't all so bad. It's not often I get to experience the calm of a snowfall like this."

Still listening to him, but ultimately distracted by my last encounter with Sylvie, I hung my necklace chain from my bottom lip, working it back and forth. She had a personal connection with a winter beast, she was fae, had wintry wings, and made delicious as fuck cupcakes. The latter had nothing to do with our potential universal tether, but I couldn't deny how even the *thought* of eating her cupcake made my mouth water.

"I'm curious how the winter king himself accidentally calls on a frost giant," the ice giant said, his arms still so humanly draped over his knees.

Groaning, I rested my head on my hand. "Would you believe me if I said a *girl?*"

The giant stared at me with those nonexistent, lifeless eyes, and somehow they remained uncomfortably judgmental. "I've been asleep for two centuries, and you still haven't found your queen?"

"And thank you for reminding me." I dragged a hand over my beard before sitting up straight. "Believe me, I've tried every solstice since the dawn of my frosty existence."

"You said a girl. Does that mean you found her? Here?" The giant pointed at the ground.

Sylvie had been so bright and full of life that first day I met her in the bakery. She was so eager to please and use her magic to make me feel better without knowing anything about me. So damn *nice*.

"It's complicated," I answered through a snarl. "I'm not sure a being such as yourself who doesn't procreate nor *love* anything could understand."

The giant shifted, making tiny flecks of ice fall from his shoulders. "That's hurtful. But true."

"She just doesn't seem right for me, but everything in my bones is telling me—" I'd been mid-declaration, waving my hands around for extra emphasis, and paused when I considered my audience.

I'm talking to a frost giant. This was a new low.

"I may not understand, but it seems to me like you are hiding out here." The frost giant raised his arms.

Standing, I cut a line through my hair with my hand. "I am not. I'm—*thinking*."

"Why don't you go think in town? You think I am so naïve because I do not possess a heart, but even I know you are not used to being around so many others that do. All you have is a polar bear, servants, and townsfolk."

My jaw had fallen slack at his well-articulated advice. Frost giants had only ever destroyed anything in the path you set them on or ate an exorbitant number of fish in preparation for their deep sleeps. I'd never talked with one, let alone for this long. This one seemed different somehow.

"Perhaps your summoning wasn't an accident after all, giant." Referencing the woods, I used my magic to build an ice cave. "Feel free to stay here as long as you like."

The frost giant turned to look at his new home and bowed to me. "I am humbled, your majesty."

After bowing my head, I gazed through the trees where, in the distance, the Arcane Cove Plaza beckoned me. The idea of the scorching heat raging in every establishment had me regretting it already, but the giant had a point. If I wanted to see if this could work—*really* work—I had to understand why she enjoyed this place so much.

Given Finneas was about the only one I could consider a friend, I headed for his pub. Nighttime had settled in the air and sky, making the place far more active since the last time I visited. I immediately moved to my corner table, but two beings already occupied it. Sweat beaded on my forehead, and I stalked for the bar, grabbing a corner stool the farthest from the hearth.

"Hey, hey, welcome back. Whiskey and ice?" Finneas smiled broadly.

He remembered my drink order? How—cozy and welcoming.

"Please, Finneas. Thanks."

Moments later, two glass tumblers appeared in front of me, and Finneas leaned his arms on the bar top. "Any luck with Sylvie?"

This guy had a memory like a steel trap.

"Too soon to say," I grumbled, swigging back half of the amber liquor.

Finneas tilted his head and pushed back, his gaze roaming my tattoo and hair. "It's not normally well-mannered to ask such things, but I get the feeling you're the type who doesn't care about all that. What exactly are you? I can't get a good read on you."

Finishing the drink, I tapped the glass. "Give me another one of those and I'll tell you."

"Deal," Finneas said, barking a hearty laugh.

I chomped on an ice cube as I scanned the pub. Several pairs of eyes kept glancing at me, some making it more evident than others, and salacious whispers to each other followed.

"Here you are." Finneas returned with a glass now filled to the brim, and he somehow sparked a grin from me at that.

Raising it in a cheerful gesture, I took a sip. "I'm Jack Frost. *That* Jack Frost."

Finneas' eyes widened, and he looked about three seconds away from "fangirling." It wouldn't be the first time, and I winced in preparation. "No shit. I know I'm a minotaur, and I know I live in Arcane Cove, but I seriously thought you were a *true* fairy tale."

"Nope. I'm as real as the Tooth Fairy." Smirking, I guzzled more whiskey. "But my winter palace is in a different celestial plane. It takes me to different realms every solstice. This was the first time it brought me *here*."

Finneas nodded before a sudden bout of excitement had him bouncing like an adolescent girl. "Was it because of Sylvie?" He gasped. "She's a winter faerie, you're winter itself. Oh my—it's so perfect." Finneas pointed a shaking finger at me. "They'd call you two *Jackie*."

Eyeing him like snakes were sprouting from his head, I tightened my grip on my tumbler. "Jackie? What? Look, look, I'm still exploring things. I don't know for sure."

Finneas frowned, absolutely deflated. "What's wrong? You don't like her?"

"I don't *hate* her," I muttered, shoving my nose in the tumbler before I said much else.

A slender beige hand slipped over my shoulder, causing my attention to shift behind me. A woman with straight black hair to her hips, dark, deep-set eyes, and nine furry white fox tails sprouting from her back stood there grinning at me. "You're new."

"I am," I started, my words coming out hesitant, and I gave Finneas the side eye.

"Duri," Finneas warned. "He won't be part of your thousand livers."

Arching a brow, I alarmedly mouthed the word "liver" to Finneas.

Duri sulked, hunching her shoulders forward. "But it's so much easier than hiding myself around a human for a hundred days."

"Have you tried venturing out of the Cove lately?" Finneas leaned on the bar, positioning himself between me and the curious female.

She let out an exaggerated sigh. "Fine. I'll *venture* somewhere tomorrow. But I'll get to tell you I told you so when it doesn't work out again."

"I can handle that," Finneas replied, his broad nose snorting when the woman, tails and all, turned to leave. "She's a kumiho."

"Can't say I've heard of that one." I stared at the door as she exited.

"Just like not everyone knows you're real." Finneas chuckled, his horns bouncing. "You want another?" He pointed at my glass.

"Please." Handing it to him, I remained transfixed.

Usually, a woman's hand on me would spark the charm and flirtation through me. But when this kumiho touched me, I grew agitated. If this hadn't been enough of a sign, I wasn't sure what else fate could throw in my lap. If I wanted to have a chance at this, I needed to *give* it one.

Eight

Sylvie

Nothing was as healing for the soul as keeping busy when your mind reeled a million miles per second. For me, that meant throwing myself into my baking—lots and lots of baking. *Sweater Weather* by The Neighbourhood blasted from my phone as I cut up prunes, dates, cranberries, and apricots. Coarsely chopped walnuts were roasting in the oven, and their earthy aroma filled the space. I threw all ingredients into a food processor along with cinnamon, cardamom, cloves, and salt. Once done, I formed the mixture into one-inch balls and placed them on parchment paper when they were the perfect size.

I'd been so hyperfocused on what I was doing that the bell chime hadn't fully registered despite hearing it faintly in the background.

"Sylvie," a female voice said. "Sylvie," they yelled louder.

Jerking to attention, I paused with a ball between two fingers and spun on my heel to face the counter. My best friend, Aella, stood there wide-eyed with her arms at her sides.

"You didn't hear the bell? Or me calling your name three times?" Her brown ringlet hair bounced when she flopped onto her heels.

47

"Sorry, Aella, I got a lot on my mind." Not wanting to lose momentum, I power-walked to the back, returning with a tray of coarse sugar.

Aella hopped onto the counter, surveying the sweet treats I had on display. "No kidding. Normally, you wait longer to make sugarplums."

"Tis the season, and all that." I rolled the fruity nut balls in sugar, then set them on a porcelain plate with hand-painted holly around its edges.

Aella rubbed one of her small fawn-like antlers before she wagged an accusatory finger at me. "This is about a guy, isn't it?"

Lunging, I shoved a sugarplum in her mouth to shut her cute little mouth up.

"Knew it," Aella said, the words coming out muffled.

"I'll have you know I'm making sugarplums early because they're decorating the plaza today, and I figured I'd bring these to brighten the holiday spirit."

Aella coughed and, without looking, I handed her a glass of water.

After guzzling half of it down, she made a loud gulping sound and hopped from the counter. "Syl, you've never helped with the decorating. And did you know your ears and wings are showing?"

My wings went taut as if they too were surprised, and I felt the tip of one ear, blinking in astonishment.

This had nothing to do with what Jack said. Nope. It did *not*.

"Or maybe, I'm turning a new leaf. Ever think of that?" Satisfied with the positioning of the sugarplums, I snagged several cinnamon-scented pine cones I'd made earlier in the week and scattered them on the plate for decoration.

Aella's face fell blank, and she folded her arms. "Who is he?"

"No one. Absolutely no one." Hoisting the platter into my palm, I bolted for the door before Aella could further her interrogation.

She used her uncanny maenad speed to beat me to the doorframe, blocking me. "Then it *is* someone. Name. Now."

I wrung my hands on the plate, making panicked squeaking sounds. "Why are you so bossy right now, Aella?"

"Because you're intrigued by someone, and for whatever reason, denying it even though I know you haven't been with anyone since before I met you. This is a big deal, and as your best friend, I demand satisfaction." Aella stomped her heeled boot against the hardwood for emphasis.

"Your satisfaction?" Smiling, I nibbled my bottom lip.

Aella let out her cute snorting laugh at that, but wiped a hand across her face to maintain her composure. "And don't think you can distract me with naughty jokes."

Sighing and fighting the urge to shove a sugarplum in *my* mouth, I relented. "His name is Jack. Happy?"

Aella's hands fell from the door. "Jack? I met a Jack the other day."

An inconvenient tinge of jealousy twisted in my stomach. More annoyingly, my first thought was that she couldn't possibly be talking about *my* Jack. Growling it away, I pinched my eyes shut. "What did he look like?"

"Uh, really, really tall. Impossibly blue eyes and spiky, snowy blonde hair like yours without the blue." Aella picked up some of my hair and examined it. "Like, exactly this color."

My eyes crisscrossed as I stared at snowy white bangs hanging over my eyelashes. Huh. *Did* I match Jack?

Batting her hand away, I blew my bangs out of my eyes. "That's him. But we're not going to talk about it. He's arrogant, self-righteous—" I trailed off because one, I couldn't think of any other negatives at the moment, and two, Aella was grinning like a devious jackal at me. "*Why* are you looking at me like that?"

"Jack and Sylvie sitting in a tree, k-i-s-s-i-n—" Aella started to sing, but I shoved another sugarplum in her mouth and shimmied past her to the sidewalk.

When the sound of her heels clicking against the cobblestones soon followed, I kept my focus forward.

"Sylvie, I'm sorry," Aella whined, catching up and walking sideways beside me. "I only want your happiness."

"Please let it go."

He said he was here for a woman who was clearly *not* me. It was already doomed to fail, and that fact further irritated me.

Aella defensively held up her palms and said nothing more as we entered the plaza. Several citizens gathered around a massive tree that rivaled the height of surrounding buildings. Candles with eternal flames hung in multiple places, along with holly, cranberries, acorns, and various carved wooden ornaments—crescent moons, pentagrams, runes, and snowflakes.

"This looks beautiful," I breathed out, standing at its base and gawking up at it.

A pixie named Flora trotted over to me with her hands curled under her chin. "Doesn't it?" Her dewy blue eyes sparkled from the flickering flames, and she continuously flapped her translucent, curved wings. "If only they could stop bickering."

She pointed at two orcs arguing and gesturing toward the top of the tree.

"Hm. Why don't you have a sugarplum and offer some to the rest of them?" I handed the plate to Flora.

"Oh dear," she said with a wistful sigh, taking the plate and jostling on her heels, making her black curly hair bounce.

"They're good. Like orgasmically good," Aella said to her, motioning for her to eat one.

Approaching the arguing and very large males, I patted my thighs, focusing on the only one I knew by name because he owned The Minty Boar. "Dagnar, what seems to be the problem?"

"Sylvie, hey, great to see you for the tree ceremony this year." Dagnar smiled, accentuating the two large tusks that protruded over his bottom lip. "We have this sun topper that Apollo made for us to use this year, but we underestimated how tall the damn tree is." He chuckled at that, but the other orc wasn't as amused.

"And someone forgot to bring a ladder," he yelled to the other citizens decorating the plaza fountain and lights with pine garland.

As if providing an answer, my wings furiously flapped behind me. Though Flora too possessed wings, she was far too tiny to lift the topper with her. I gestured for them to hand it over. "I can do it."

"Your wings," Dagnar said, staring in awe at them, shimmering with ice and snow. "I honestly forgot you had them."

"I did a little too, but have recently been inspired to show them off more."

And not because of the way Jack looked at them, mesmerized. This was for *me*.

With the sun topper in hand, I marveled at the actual sun vapors floating around its circular golden base. Using the power of my wings, I flew to the top and gently rested the topper there, hovering backward to gaze at the completed tree in all its glory from the best seat in the house.

"How does it look from down there?" I yelled, still hovering and staring at the animated miniature sun atop the tree.

"Gorgeous," Flora beamed.

Aella made some form of an "ooo" sound while Dagnar offered a thumbs up. The other orc waved his hands at it, sneered, and walked away.

Letting myself slowly float to the ground, I paused to watch the Arcane Cove citizens happily enjoying my sugarplums. They were laughing, chatting, and humming various popular holiday melodies. The heartwarming sight brought a comforting smile to my lips, and I started humming a song, not realizing which one had come to my mind first.

Aella leaned toward me and off-key sang, "Jack Frost nipping at your nose."

"Don't make me shove an entire blueberry muffin in your mouth next." I glared at her.

Aella grimaced. "But I hate blueberries."

"I know," I replied, flashing a wicked grin.

Aella playfully smacked me on the shoulder, and we threw ourselves into a childish, frantic game of batting each other's hands and giggling.

"Well, I for one think it's absolutely beautiful," a male's voice said, deep as the Earth's core.

Aella and I froze, our fingers interlaced, and I peered around her, instantly hating myself for the disappointment that trickled over me like hot fudge drizzle. It wasn't Jack. It was Thor.

Aella snorted and tossed her hair over one shoulder. "Were you talking about the tree or me, Norseman?"

"Actually—" Thor's bright eyes glinted, his auburn hair accentuated by the candles' flames. "—no offense, but I was referring to Sylvie *and* the tree."

Aella made an exaggerated circle with her head and chin, mouthing the word "okay" before she spun away. "In that case, I'll go build a snowman with Flora." She grabbed my shoulder as she passed, pulling me closer. "This could be an excellent distraction from you know who. Take it, Sylvie."

Taking another glance at Thor beaming at me, his tanned, carved arm muscles bulged from underneath the brown leather vest he wore.

Yes, Sylvie was right.

Approaching him with hands folded behind my back, I chewed the inside of my cheek, suddenly feeling like a shy schoolgirl once I'd gotten closer. "Beautiful, huh? You've been in the bakery several times, and I don't recall you ever saying that."

Thor rubbed an uncomfortable hand at the back of his neck, making that bicep bounce. "I thought about it. Just never said it. You're a different breed of female, Sylvie. Not to mention, I've never seen your wings before."

My stomach gurgled at his choice of words, and my wings folded back as if to hide from him. "A different *breed*?"

"Apologies, that probably didn't come out the way I intended. I only meant that you're a genuinely sweet person." Thor wrapped his hand around the hammer pendant hanging from his neck. "I never said anything because I figured you wouldn't ever be interested in a brute like me."

My wings flared out again. "And *are* you a brute?"

"To a certain extent, yes." Thor chuckled and made his golden hammer appear, twirling it by its handle. "I do fight frost giants and sea serpents regularly. Not to mention I regularly drink mead from a curved horn."

Smiling sheepishly, I found myself twisting my foot on a pebble. "Your honesty goes a long way, I'd reckon."

"Yeah? Could I convince you to have a drink with me? Or coffee or tea?" Thor laughed and nudged his head at The Minty Boar café.

Jack's face flashed through my mind, a disapproving scowl distorting his features. Why should I care what Jack thought when he was here for another woman? It was enough to have me offering my arm to Thor. The Norse god of thunder led me to the café where we settled into a small table with two chairs.

This was precisely what I needed to forget all about Jack and his mysterious haughtiness. As far as I was concerned, Jack could hit the road.

Nine

Jack

It should be simple. I'd tell her that I wished to show her the true extent of my power, and as a winter faerie, she'd be in awe. Kissing her could be a tell-all if we *were* true mates—the reactions our bodies would have from the connection—impulses that went beyond lust and attraction. I'd been going over what to say to her as I trekked back to town, miming and stammering.

When I exited the forest, the plaza came into full view, a solstice tree now standing at the center of it. Several citizens were busy decorating the street lamps with holly and garland. Pausing at the tree's base, I scanned the ornaments, a small smile cresting my lips at the snowflakes.

"Jack?" A female voice asked.

The maenad I'd met briefly leaned in front of me, her fingers steepled.

"Yes?" A crease formed between my eyes as I stared at her.

"Are you looking for Sylvie?"

I took a step away. "How did you know that?"

"She's my best friend." Aella shrugged and rubbed the tip of her nose that'd gone rosy from the chilly air.

Pausing, I stood upright. "Have you seen her?"

"Yup." Aella pointed behind me and clicked her heels together. "The Minty Boar."

"Thanks." I started to walk toward the café but glanced back at the maenad sucking her lips into her mouth as if she was trying not to tell me something.

What I saw through the café windows made my blood boil. The instantaneous rage had me seeing red for the first time in my ethereal life, and the thoughts racing through my brain were borderline ridiculous. There was Sylvie, laughing and touching the forearm of some other male with red hair. Those should be *my* laughs, those fleeting touches should be *my* touches. Who the fuck did this guy think he was?

Without thinking, without any preparation whatsoever, I stormed into the café, bringing a snowy current with me that wafted from the doorway. The closest patrons shivered and frantically reached for their coats. The roaring fire in the hearth died out with one flick of my finger.

The auburn-haired man sat back in his chair and furrowed his brow at me, ice crystals already forming on the hair surrounding his mouth.

Sylvie, unaffected by my wintry anger, turned in her chair, gaping when she saw it was me. "Jack? What the seven hells are you doing?"

Ignoring her question, I stalked toward the table, fanning my palm at the male stranger, relishing the sight of his face turning a light shade of blue. "Who *are* you?"

"Jack," Sylvie yelled, but my focus stayed on the red-haired buffoon.

The man gripped the table, fighting back some, but not all, of my power. "Thor. God of—"

"Yes," I started, clenching my hand into a fist and pumping more ice through his veins. It wouldn't kill him, but it sure as shit didn't feel good. "I've heard of you. Do you often fiddle with things that don't belong to you, Norseman?"

"Belong?" Sylvie roared, pushing to her feet. "Jack, stop it."

Thor looked between us, the shivers becoming uncontrollable now, his lips turning sapphire. "I—I didn't know."

"Jack," Sylvie shouted again, her hand slipping over my bicep this time.

The reaction was immediate. My blood usually ran cold. I *breathed* the cold as I always had. The moment Sylvie touched me, though, a swirling warmth pooled in my stomach and chest—a comforting heat that didn't make me sweat or feel like my insides were melting. It *thawed* me. Sylvie's lips parted, her wings fluttering faster now, and she stared at the spot where our skin made contact. When she pulled away, still gazing at her hand, the chill washed over me again, and I doused my power, letting it seep through the cracks of the building and out the door.

"Sylvie," I whispered, a snowball-sized knot forming in my throat, making it hard to speak. "We need to talk."

A tortured wrinkle formed in Sylvie's forehead, and she shook her head. "Talk? After that caveman display I just witnessed?"

Thor let out a relieved breath, his grip loosening on the table. He had the good sense to keep his mouth shut.

"You don't understand. That's precisely *why* I need to talk to you."

I was seconds away from losing her; I could hear it in her tone and see it in the steely glare she gave me. I'd been searching for so, so long, and I couldn't afford the luxury of my ego.

"Please," I croaked, an unintended plea dancing in my gaze.

Sylvie searched my face, surveying my posture before sighing. "We can talk in the bakery."

The uncomfortable feeling of the heat I'd associated with the bakery now had me kneading my arm with my thumb. "Anywhere but the bakery."

"What's wrong with the bakery?" Sylvie arched a brow and frowned as if insulted by my request.

This was not how I envisioned this unavoidable conversation going.

"The heat. I—" Rubbing the back of my neck from the vulnerable itch clawing at my throat, I locked my eyes with hers. "—I can't *stand* it."

Sylvie gave a weak grin, a pitying expression that struck an ache in my skull. "The ovens aren't on, Jack."

"What in *Styx* happened in here?" Dagnar asked, entering his café where snow still littered the floorboards and the fire no longer warmed the space.

Ashamed, another first for me in eons, I tightened my jaw and used my magic to summon the snow, absorbing it into my skin. "Apologies. I have no way of relighting the fire, but—"

"It's fine. Nothing a torch can't handle. I wouldn't live in Arcane Cove if I never expected weird and supernatural things to occur." Dagnar chuckled and moved past us as if nothing had happened.

This place was so strange. I couldn't wrap my head around it, let alone its inhabitants.

"Come on, Jack," Sylvie beckoned, standing at the open door. She glanced at Thor with a sympathetic smile; and that same rage sent a blinding blizzard through my veins.

Growling, I stormed for the door before impulses overtook all sensibility, and I followed Sylvie to the bakery.

No sooner had we entered than she pulled down the blinds and whirled on her heels to face me with sternly crossed arms. "What the hell was that, Jack? I'm allowed to have coffee with someone, especially when you and I are nothing to each other. We're not even friends."

Grimacing at her words, I propped myself on the counter for purchase. "That's where you're wrong, faerie."

"Oh? Do enlighten me, Mr. Frost."

I drummed my fingers before casting my gaze on her. "We're *mates*."

Sylvie's eyes blinked, her wings fanning in and out. "Mates? That's not possible." She pressed a hand to her forehead and rubbed the tip of one ear.

I couldn't have been sure what her reaction would be, but relaying my exact words from the first day we met threw me off guard. "I thought that at first, too, but why do *you* think that?"

"They told me I could never be someone's mate," Sylvie whispered, her eyes glazing over.

The hurt in her voice had my gut churning, and a sudden compulsion to pulverize whoever put that asinine thought in her head overwhelmed me. "Who told you that?"

She licked her lips and busied herself straightening boxes on a display shelf. "If it's all the same to you, I'm not quite ready to get that deep with you yet."

Yet. She said *yet*.

"Fair enough." I stopped trying to get nearer to her for fear I might somehow spook her on this very thin ice we treaded. "We hardly know each other."

"We *don't* know each other, Jack," Sylvie replied haughtily, her hand falling to her side.

"Right," I breathed out, my mind muddied by the desperation of finally finding my mate, only for it to become so complicated. I glanced at the clock on the wall as if it represented my dwindling time here.

"If you were so unsure about this yourself before, what changed suddenly that you believe it to be true?" Sylvie's eyes stayed fixed on the display case, unable to meet my gaze.

"The moment I saw you with him, an uncontrollable possessiveness consumed me. For a moment, I wasn't in control of my own actions. That's never happened to me." Staring at the warbles in the wooden floor, I combed my beard with my fingers.

Sylvie shifted from one foot to the other, and for a second, I thought I had her, but she threw her hands in the air, shrieking in frustration. "What am I supposed to think about all of this? Hm?"

There wasn't a way for me to answer that. All I could do was keep convincing her that what I was saying was true.

"When you touched me, I could tell from your expression you felt something too. What was it?" I pushed from the counter, cautiously moving closer to her.

That delicious heat I'd felt from her. I wanted to experience it again. It was mere meters from me. One simple touch.

Sylvie had been chewing on her thumbnail, a hand propped on her hip, and she snapped her attention my way, her eyes glistening. "A blissful chill. Like I could stand naked in a blizzard in below freezing temperature and it'd be the most comfortable

I've ever been."

The mere thought of her doing just that had my dick going ice hard, and I shifted my stance.

"That's something *I* can do." I pressed a hand to my chest, edging closer to her. Reaching out my hand, I caught Sylvie's shimmering violet gaze. "Let me show you my powers."

Sylvie first looked at my hand, then back to my eyes, curling her fists to her chest like I'd really nip at her or something. "I'm pretty sure I've already witnessed them." Smirking, she turned away from me.

Staying put, I re-emphasized my awaiting palm. "No. You haven't."

Her enchanting gaze returned to me, intrigue and amusement dancing there.

"And maybe, you'll feel inclined to show me yours as well," I added.

Sylvie's bottom lip quivered and her wings quickly fanned—whether it was from excitement or trepidation, I couldn't tell. "What makes you think I have powers?"

She was afraid. Why?

"Because you're my mate, Sylvie." When her face still looked uncertain, I called on my winter magic, coiling a small amount of snowfall to land in my palm. "You don't have to show me if you don't wish to, but I'd love to see what you can do."

Sylvie concentrated on my hand for so long I thought for sure she was mulling over a way to turn me down, but as she continued to do, she surprised me with, "Fine."

A relieved, chilly breath pushed from my lungs, and I stood there with my palm in the air, still, waiting. "Fine."

"On one condition." She held up a single finger, her wings

flapping erratically.

My own intrigue bubbled excitedly in my stomach, and I quirked a small smile. "I'm listening."

"You need to catch me first," she challenged, whisking open the bakery door and taking flight, already heading for the woods.

Blinking in disbelief, I allowed her to get a head start, using my spiraling snow magic to make an icy trail leading out of the bakery and into the forest. Time was of the essence now that I had found my fate, and the future of my kingdom fell not only on this winter faerie's shoulders but on my ability to not *fuck* it up.

Ten

Sylvie

That crisp, icy, velvety sensation that tantalized my skin when he'd touched me did traitorous things to my mind, but mostly to my body. It was apparent how incredibly addictive it could become—Jack Frost's wintry embrace. I wanted to think I would keep my wits about me, not to let the idea of him being *mine* cloud my judgment, but as I flew freely through the woods for the first time in years, I wasn't sure I *wanted* to be sensible. He chastised me for hiding what I was, and he was right. Arcane Cove allowed me to be myself in my own skin, to be *proud* that I was a winged, winter fae. Damn them all, my own *kind*, who'd convinced me to sulk in the shadows.

The chilly air wisped through my hair as I pushed my wings to their limit. The last time I exhausted them like this, I was playing tag with the other kids who ran on foot because I was the only one in our village with wings. Faint sounds of shifting ice soon emanated behind me, and I had to bite back the smile begging at my lips before peering over my shoulder.

Jack, with his hands folded behind his back, calmly skated

on a pathway made of ice, the magic pulsing from his feet. He whistled *The Christmas Song* and turned backward, gliding in figure eights now while keeping with my speed.

"You could at least make that look a tad more challenging for you," I argued, attempting to mask the discomfort burning in my shoulders from wing use.

Jack only grinned, those sparkling, ice-blue eyes reeling me in like an impending avalanche. "And you should watch out for that tree." He poked his thumb behind him, darting out of the way.

A wide birch tree appeared out of nowhere from the blurred, snowy drifts, and I yelped, turning in time to avoid impaling myself on its trunk. The sudden change of direction and my inexperience with flying had me in a frantic spin of barrel rolls until I plummeted headfirst into a snow bank.

Huffing, I pulled my face from the powdery flakes and glared at Jack through my disheveled, wet hair. He was *smirking* at me. "Think you could've given more notice?"

"I honestly thought you'd avoid it without issue given—" Jack turned his hands into little wings, hooking his thumbs together and flapping. "—have you not used them in a while? At all? I get why you hid them in public, but—"

I shook the flakes from my hair and shoulders, my wings bristling to rid themselves of the snow weighing them down. "*Do you get it? Do you?*" Sighing, I sulked in defeat on the ground, my shoulders slumping. Even the cold wetness from the snow seeping through my pants wasn't enough to jar me from my pity party. "This was a bad idea."

"Which part, faerie?" Jack's hand extended to me. "You ending up on your ass in a snow bank, or giving us a chance?"

It was a simple gesture—an outstretched palm to help me stand. Some would have even referred to it as gentlemanly, but with us, so much rested in that act of his. He knew what would happen if our skin touched. Surely, how I made him feel was as euphoric for him as it was for me. Had he wanted to experience it again, or was he genuinely offering his assistance?

"I never said I was necessarily giving us a chance." Deciding to ignore his hand, for now, I hoisted myself up and brushed off my butt. "You wanted to show me your powers, and here I am. Was the Iceman routine it? Are we done?"

Jack frowned, a deep scowl following, and his hands coiled into fists. "Iceman? Who is that? I don't like him already."

Holding up a hand in a halting gesture, I shook my head and bit the inside of my cheek to hide my grin. "Before you go freezing him to death in some form of icy pissing contest, he's a fictional character from *X-Men*."

Jack's glare softened, but he still stood rigid like he had zero idea what I was talking about.

"Never mind. Anyway, are we done?" My wings folded back as if to tell me *we* were not going anywhere.

"Sit down," Jack commanded, his hands loosening, but a steely, animalistic glint flashed in his gaze.

My body wasn't sure whether to slap him or kiss him with a tone like that.

"Excuse me?" My voice came out far raspier than I would have preferred. There wasn't nearly enough anger in it either.

"Sit down," he repeated, dropping his voice, gravel coating the words now.

Something hit the back of my thighs, forcing me to sit, and

I gasped at the sight of two armrests made out of ice appearing beneath me. Gulping, I softly settled into the ice throne he'd created. My heart raced at the implication of it—try it on for size, see how it feels, *faerie*.

"There we are. I ask for five minutes without talking and with an open mind. Think you can handle that?" A sparkle flickered in his right eye, his ears perking, awaiting my answer.

"Can you?" I replied like a brat, haughtily folding my arms and bouncing in my seat.

Jack didn't seem annoyed by my antics. Instead, he chuckled and scratched his chin through his beard. "Five minutes starting from *now*."

Crossing my legs at the ankle, I gulped down the sand coating my throat at the sight of him waiting for me to be quiet, to pay attention. Keeping my word, I gave a soft nod.

Jack's eyes went from inhumanly blue to pure ice, a devious smile cresting his lips before a spiraling snow flurry started at his feet and worked its way to his head. He disappeared. Sitting up straight, I gripped the armrests and looked for him.

Was this a joke?

It started subtly at first, the rhythmic sound of hooves pounding the frozen soil. I willed myself to stay put, to show Jack I wasn't weak or vulnerable simply because I'd grown used to hiding myself. Ice horses plunged through the trees in a stampede, their breaths huffing from their snouts in white vapors. Nerves prickled my spine, but I cemented myself to the seat. The equines charged toward me, splitting like a seam when they neared the throne, running past. Jack rode one horse, his hair and beard glistening with ice crystals now, a white cloak with fur draping over his shoulders, intricate silver-twig embroidery sewn through it.

That same confident and satisfied smile graced his lips. The sight of it made my stomach tighten, and it swooshed into my core, my grip tightening on the throne, cracking the ice. Now several feet in front of me, Jack back-flipped from the horse, the stampede turning into sparkling silver trails of magic and snow. When Jack landed, he swooped his arm first left then right, raising icy spires from the ground, zooming past the trees and into the grey clouds. They morphed into pillars one would see outfitting a castle. He swiveled on his heel, the skin on his hands replaced with smoking ice. Jack's power conjured in his palm, spiraling ivory magic with a never-ending cascade of snowflakes. He flicked his hand at a birch tree between us, dozens of icy spikes launching into it like throwing knives.

Jack shot his palms forward, an ice trail forming over the blades of frosty grass, leading under my chair. He circled his hands around the other, magic curling around the throne's base, my legs, and arms. His power lifted me until he, too, rose, his head in line with my knees. I pinned my calves against the seat, not daring to look down at how high we'd gotten. When the seat stopped, it towered over the tree line, and all of Arcane Cove was in full view.

Jack slowly appeared before me, crackles and twinkles sparking from his wintry magic, surrounding us, supporting us. One arm draped across his back, and he bent forward, a rose made of ice appearing between two fingers, shimmering with bright blue flakes. Grinning, his canines somehow looking larger and sharper now, he held it out to me.

My throat tightened, sinuses stinging, and I couldn't be certain why straight away, but tears *welled* in my eyes. I swallowed, trying to force them back, but they weren't having it, one escaping and rolling down my cheek, freezing against my skin.

Jack frowned, and his gaze snapped to the iced teardrop. "What did I do, Sylvie?"

If I weren't holding back a sob, that question may have made me laugh. How uncanny for him to assume it was *he* who did something.

"Nothing. Your powers are *extraordinary*. They're beyond anything I could've imagined," I croaked, the words broken and strained.

"I—" Jack started, the ice covering his face melting, followed by the wind taking the rose away in a snowy drift. "—don't understand."

Sniffling, I gripped the edge of my seat. "I'm nothing compared to you, Jack. This? All of what you've done? I'm not nearly this powerful."

Jack said nothing, only continued to stare at me, and slowly, we descended.

"You know what I can do?" I rolled my shoulders back and sat straighter.

Jack remained silent and calmly folded his hands in front of him, listening to me intently.

"I can use my magic—" Conjuring some of it, I let it swirl my knuckles and collect in the air between us. Jack wiggled his fingers through the tiny snowflakes, his ears perking. "—to lace food with what beings need to uplift them. The spells could last an hour, a day, or a week. I can fly, and the cold, *winter*, makes me feel like I could blanket an entire village with my magic."

Some of my power still settled on Jack's fingers, and a small smile lifted at the corner of his lips at the sight of it.

Pushing to my feet, I held my arms out at my sides before letting them flop. "That's *all* I can do. You're so powerful, Jack. You clearly need someone who can match your speed, and that's *not* me."

Jack closed the distance between us so quickly he must've used his magic, and my chin was within his grasp, thumb and forefinger holding me captive, his cerulean gaze locking me in. "Do you think so little of yourself to believe your magic is any less worthy than mine, Sylvie?"

The chill flowing into me from him made my knees wobbly, and he snaked an arm around my waist to steady me. Jack's eyes closed for a moment, a carnal moan bubbling in his throat before he looked at me again.

"I can't compare to you," I whispered, nuzzling against his touch now.

Jack shook his head left to right, deliberately slow, making faint *tsking* sounds. "Mates aren't supposed to be a comparison to each other, but a balance." He wiggled my chin still within his grasp. "What do you think *this* is?"

There was that word again. Mates.

Gulping because I'd probably regret it later, I pulled away from him. Fear of the unknown, terror at the idea of such a significant change, and skepticism from Jack's sudden change in demeanor had me reeling back. "I should go."

Jack's hand stayed extended as if I'd return to his touch. When I didn't, he curled his fingers against his palm and let it fall. "*Should* you? Or is it because you're scared?"

I wrapped my arms around myself, my wings fanning so erratically they kicked up snow behind me. "Both," I said in a cracked whisper.

"I won't stop you." Jack pointed at me. "But just know, I've searched centuries for you, and don't intend on giving up that easily, faerie."

Whether I should've taken that as a grand declaration or a threat was still unclear, but either way, I believed him. Shuffling backward, I kept my gaze locked with his. Jack stood motionless, watching me disappear into the woodlands' thick mass of snow-covered trees. When he was no longer in sight, sobs overcame me, and I bolted for home. But I didn't run, I *flew*.

Eleven

Jack

"Well, shit," I mumbled, leaning against my polar bear with my ass on the ground. "Now what?"

Nanok huffed, pushing me forward only for me to flop against his side again. "What? You saw the whole thing. I pulled out all the stops, and she *still* ran away."

Nanok lowered his head near my cheek and snorted, the air from his nose wafting and misting my cheek.

Frowning at him, I wiped it away. "Really?"

A sparking chime sounded in my mind, and I groaned.

"Of all the times—" Snarling, I swiped my hand in the air, creating a one-way window with a view of my realm. "Yes, Diedre?"

Her face appeared in a ripple, skin as pale as snow, eyes like rubies. Her hair hung in stringy grey tendrils, black tar leaking from her eyes down her cheeks and disappearing before it rolled from her chin. She adjusted her onyx crown, her pointy dagger-like fingernails catching the light of a sconce overhead.

"You actually answered. Color me surprised," she mused, her voice thick with the old English accent she loved to use.

Sighing, I hitched my knees and rested my forearms on them. "You left me no choice in that regard."

Diedre tapped a nail against her midnight lips and cackled. "Oh, that's right. How silly of me."

"Does this waste of my time have a point?"

Diedre was the Snow Queen of another region of my realm. I'd never made any move to overthrow her and take her lands, and for centuries, it had been a peaceful co-existence. This was until she gained word that I still had no Queen of my own—that I still hadn't found my mate. She cursed me because of it—an actual *hex*.

"Word in the clouds, Jakzair, is that you found *her*." Diedre's gaze turned predatory, her nails clacking together.

Sitting up straight, I glared at her, Nanok growling and baring his teeth behind me, sensing my sudden aggression. "You will not stop me. You can't."

"True, I can't whisk myself to where you are, but I do have other ways, darling. Besides, all she needs to do is *reject* you." Diedre chuckled, deep and sinister, her body swiveling in impending delight.

Rejection. The idea of it had a proverbial knife twisting in my gut. It was a distinct possibility, but I couldn't fathom it. Didn't want to imagine it.

"She won't," I clipped, tightening my jaw.

Diedre cackled at that, motioning to someone out of view. "That has always been your greatest asset and largest flaw. Such *confidence*."

Frustration chilled my veins to frozen spikes, and I punched the ground. "You have your kingdom, Diedre. I've never threatened to take it. What use do you have of mine?"

Diedre received a silver goblet and kissed the air in thanks to whoever had brought it to her. "One, yours is far larger, and two—" Her demeanor changed in an instant, an angered glare distorting her already grotesque features. "—you're allowed passage to other realms every solstice. Do you have any idea what I wouldn't give to see the Ice Spires, or the Alps?"

Rolling my eyes because I'd seen them both, I sighed. "They're overrated."

Diedre took a long sip from her drink, curling her elongated and thin fingers around the cup. "All the more reason I cannot wait to witness you fail, *Jack Frost*."

"Get used to where you are because that's not happening."

It couldn't happen. There *was* a spark between Sylvie and me, and I could tell from her reactions that my touch made her melt as much as hers did for me. How could she deny feeling that way forever?

"We shall see. Maybe you should scare her away with that brutish animal you keep company with." Diedre chuckled into her goblet. "Ta-ta for now, lover boy." Her hand swiped upward, making the magical tether disappear.

Nanok growled and swatted his massive paws where Diedre had just been, not at all happy with her insult toward him.

Huh. Sylvie obviously liked animals if she kept that stag around. I didn't often—no, I *never* introduced anyone to Nanok, but if I wished to have her at my side for all eternity, that meant with him too.

"Actually, it might not be such a bad idea, old friend." Rising, I dusted myself off and scratched my polar bear's head. "I need you to be on your cutest, cuddliest behavior, hm?"

Nanok's face fell blank, and he grunted.

"Oh, stop it. Like you don't enjoy belly scratches." Motioning for him to follow, I made for the woods, my nose poised for

Sylvie's scent.

Nanok perked up at this, his fluffy tail swaying and his ears folding back against his head.

Sylvie's scent was unmistakable with its sweet aroma and fruity undertones. She was in her cottage, Fintan standing with his head through one of the open windows. Nanok walked calmly by my side, and as we neared the opposite window, I held my hand out behind me, signaling for him to hold back. The bear grunted but acquiesced. Peering from the window's side just like I had that first day at the bakery, I stole a glimpse at my angelic faerie in her element. She buzzed around her quaint kitchen, flour smattering her cheeks, and the most blissful buttery smells wafted from the stone hearth oven.

Grinning at the window left ajar, I rested my forearms on the pane, my chin atop them. "Funny, I figured you'd prefer the space of your bakery for this." I knew I wouldn't scare her because she'd have sensed me the moment I stood outside her home. And I knew this because we *were* mates.

Sylvie paused halfway to the oven with a tray of star-shaped dough pieces lined on a tray and didn't look at me at first. "What do you want, Jack?"

"A chance. I've told you this, Sylvie. I understand why you're scared. I, too, have spent centuries alone."

Nanok nudged at my arm, and I pushed on his head for him to stay out of sight.

"You don't understand if you think the fear comes from being attached to someone after being alone." The light dimmed from Sylvie's eyes before she marched to the oven, shoved the tray into it, and slammed the door shut.

"So, you *have* been alone? There hasn't been anyone recently?" I scratched the tip of my ear, skirting around the real question I wanted to ask.

Tell me the names of every male who has ever laid a hand on you so I can freeze them from the inside out and toss them over a cliff.

"Really, Jack? Fishing for bed post numbers?" A tiny, microscopic smile edged on my faerie's lips, and it was enough to catapult me into action.

Chuckling, I drummed my hands on the wood and opened the window farther. "Is that what you call it?"

Sylvie made a hard swallow and turned to face the counter, leaning her palms on it.

"Sylvie?" A peculiar concern tore at my gut. The sensation inconveniently traveled its way up to my frozen heart, cracking it. "We *can* explore this if you're willing to open up to me."

Sylvie's wings spread wide before fanning slowly—in and out like a soothing trance. "It's just—" Her words cut short, eyes bulging from her skull. She stared at the window above the kitchen counter, where a giant white bear head poked its nosy black snout through the crack in the fucking window. "Oh my— is that a—" She backed away, trembling and tripping over a chair.

"Nanok," I barked. "I told you to *stay*." Sprinting to the front of the house, Nanok backed away and slumped on his butt, his back legs kicking out to the sides.

The cottage's door creaked open, and Sylvie's head appeared. "Is that a polar bear, Jack?"

Sylvie's stag curiously trotted to Nanok, his antlers poised ready so that the bear wouldn't get ideas that he was his next meal.

"Yes, this is Nanok. And he doesn't have stag on his dinner

menu. Isn't that right, boy?" I furrowed my brow at my furry white friend.

Nanok yawned, baring his ridiculously huge teeth that looked far more intimidating than he was to those who threatened him.

Sylvie gave a brightened smile. The sight of it made my chest swell. *I* put that there.

Nanok shoved his head into my back as if he could hear my thoughts.

Fine. Nanok put it there, but he was *my* polar bear.

"You're very handsome, Nanok," Sylvie cooed, stroking a hesitant hand over Nanok's back. "This is Fintan," she added, referring to the stag.

Fintan snorted and scraped his hoof on the ground like he didn't trust us yet. That would make two of them, I reckoned.

Sylvie used her nails to scratch behind Nanok's ear, which sent his back paw into a vibrating frenzy. "Is that the spot?" She grinned again, her striking violet eyes sparking to life from the glistening white snow surrounding us.

Petting Nanok with her, I edged closer. "Sylvie, why are you afraid?" When she immediately went on the defensive, I held a palm up. "I'm not asking to pressure you, I'm simply trying to understand."

Nanok's eyes practically rolled into the back of his head, and he curled into a ball before lying on his back and sprawling for her to reach his stomach.

With Nanok's fur keeping her relaxed, Sylvie smiled warmly and sank to her knees to scratch over his ribs. With a deep sigh, she panned her gaze to me. "I'm different from others of my kind. There are no other winter faeries in existence, which is why I hadn't known what to call myself for the longest time."

Nodding, I knelt beside her, tickling between Nanok's toes because I knew he hated that. He couldn't have *all* the fun. "And fae with wings are also rare."

Faeries.

"Yes. My power scared my people. I lived in the mountains with them in Norway. They tolerated me through my adolescence, but when I accidentally caused an avalanche, nearly destroying half our village, they cast me out. It was an accident. My magic reacted to my emotions." Sylvie turned her face away from me, concentrating on running her fingers through Nanok's fur.

Fintan appeared at her side, nuzzling his head against her shoulder, feeling her discomfort.

"You've been holding back," I gruffly whispered.

Curiosity for what she could really do brightened my very being.

Sylvie licked her lips and settled back on her haunches. "I've been doing it for so long, I'm not even sure what my powers are anymore. Something tells me that my connection with you—" Her gorgeous eyes lifted to mine again. "—it'd *unleash* it."

"Why is that something to fear, Sylvie? That sounds, what did you call my power? Extraordinary?"

She furiously shook her head. "Because I hurt people, Jack. I accidentally *killed* some of them. I don't want to risk that again."

It all made perfect sense now.

Taking one of her hands between both of mine, I pulsed my magic through her skin. "You'd have me to help you navigate it. I wouldn't let that happen."

Sylvie's shoulder had relaxed to my touch, her body going damn near boneless before she snatched her hand away. "There's more."

I stared at my palms, the act of her pulling away from me repeatedly stinging the more she did it.

"I haven't fully been with a male, with *anyone*," she confessed, the words coming out strained and jittery.

Fuck. I should not have been as elated to hear this, but here I was being just that.

How to navigate that without coming across as an absolute dick.

"So, you're a uh—" The word "virgin" has rendered Jack Frost speechless.

Sylvie clapped her hands to her face. "Yes. I mean, I've done other things, but—"

And there went the possessive, jealous rage again.

"—the one time I tried he—he only got so far before—"

Curiosity had me leaning forward, waiting for her to finish. "What happened?"

"*It* got frostbite." Sylvie pressed her palms harder against her cheeks. "I never dared to try again."

The thought had me adjusting my pants. Served the asshole right, but also that poor bastard.

Delicately removing her hands from her face, I held them and flashed a grin with a bit of fang showing. "That wouldn't happen to me, faerie. And I'd be willing to stake my cock on it."

Sylvie pushed out a small laugh, and she rose, the sun peeking through the grey clouds above the trees framing her in a wintry halo. She still held my hands, and I remained on my knees in front of her, staring up at those icy blue wings and imagining how a crown would look atop her snowy white hair. Hair that I hadn't noticed until now *matched* mine. It all made too much sense to deny.

"What a queen you'll be," I whispered.

Sylvie's head moved, now in full view and no longer framed by the sun. Her hands yanked from mine, and her expression was anything but pleasant. "What? You make it sound like this is a done deal. Are you so sure of yourself that you think this is in the bag?"

Here I thought I knew females only to find out they're an absolute enigma.

"I thought it was a compliment. Is it not? You'd be royalty, have a palace, a kingdom, power—"

Sylvie cut me off by pointing a stern finger behind me. "Please leave, Jack."

Nanok harumphed and stood, lightly bumping his head against Sylvie's arm.

"You're a good boy, Nanok." She ruffled Nanok's neck.

Standing and rolling my shoulders, I paused long enough for Sylvie to flash me with a gaze I could only describe as confused, hurt, and still just a small glimmer of hope there.

"Alright. Have a good evening, faerie."

Motioning for Nanok to follow, I turned on my heel to walk away as she asked. Winning her over would take more than promises of grandeur and a shared pet polar bear. It'd clearly take proof that her soul was solidly safe in my hands.

Twelve

Sylvie

"What is *wrong* with him?" I fumed, a wicker basket secured on my forearm as I perused various flowers in Flora's shop, *Flora and Fauna*.

While the flora portion of the title was pretty obvious, given my pixie best friend's name as well as it being a floral shop, the fauna came from the numerous pets she let roam free in the store during hours—a couple of cats, a small dog, a raven, a miniature pig, and a chicken. You'd think they would cause chaos and poop everywhere, but Flora had them well-trained. They brought smiles to customers, and regulars looked forward to visiting with them.

Flora stood near the cash register, arranging a wintry bouquet of white roses, blue delphinium, mini daisies, and feather willow eucalyptus. "Do you want me to support you no matter what, or is this a moment you'd like my honest opinion?"

I twirled twigs of cranberries between two fingers, holding them up to the light before adding them to my haul. Sighing, I turned to face her, propping the basket on one hip. "I'm probably going to regret this, but be honest with me."

Flora dusted her hands, nodded, and pressed her palms on the counter. "I think you're blowing this out of proportion." Her small wings fluttered erratically, a finger raising as soon as I opened my mouth to defend myself. "You asked for honesty, so hush up and listen to it, Syl."

Holding back the urge to stomp my foot like a child not getting their way, I bit my lips together and kept quiet.

"In this situation, Jack was trying to impress a would-be mate. He was the peacock showing you his elaborately beautiful feather display." Flora plucked a peacock feather from a vase on a table surrounded by various bird feather types and waved it at me. "You *were* impressed, were you not?"

Yes. And that look on his face as he used his magic—so confident, so powerful, so utterly and completely in *control.*

Tracing my fingers over a poinsettia, I gave a nonchalant shrug. "Maybe."

"Yes," Flora shouted, making the cats screech and scurry under the counter. "Say yes, because you *were.*"

I clutched the basket to my chest like Flora was about to shoot fireballs from her eyes at me. "Why are you being so mean? You're *never* mean."

"I'm not being mean. This is called tough love. Now admit it, Sylvaria." Flora slapped her hands together.

The sound made me jump, and I flopped the flower basket onto the nearest display case. "Alright, alright. Yes. It was very impressive. Happy?"

Flora tilted her head at the peacock feather before adding it to her in-progress bouquet. "Now, Jack, being the peacock in this scenario, sees that his efforts are working, and he's that much closer. His telling you what a queen you'll be is his reaction to *your* reaction, and I find it completely valid."

The way he commanded me to sit, to watch his "display." Recalling it had my thighs pinching together.

The skin underneath my eyes crinkled, and a peculiar tidal wave of guilt threatened to drown me. "I take it back. Tell me what I *want* to hear, Flor."

Grinning, her usual peppy demeanor back, she primped the bouquet with her palms. "Too late. Why are you so combative at the prospect of having a mate, anyway? I think it's pretty great."

Turning back to the vast array of flower selections, I jolted when I was met with a chicken cocking its head sideways and nearly upside down at me, giving a single *bawk*. "Petunia, you almost startled me out of my skin." Smiling, I patted the chicken's head. "You weren't there when Jack and I first met. He was cocky, elusive, and cold."

Handsome. Confident. That tattoo. Those *muscles*.

"Cold? You really going with that one, Syl?"

I slammed the basket back down and whirled to face her. "Okay, I need you to be at least five percent on my side."

"I am one hundred percent on your side, friend." Flora stretched over the counter, her apple cheeks going rosy from the effort. She squeezed my forearm. "And he's a butthead for being such a meanie, but he's trying to turn that around now, isn't he?"

"Sure. Now that it's convenient." I blew my bangs from my eyes and rubbed the tip of my ear.

Flora came around the corner now, taking the tiniest of steps that only a pixie could pull off. When she stood next to me, her head was in line with my boobs, and she gave me a side hug, her temple pressing against the side of them. "Who hurt you, sweetie? I don't recall you having anyone recently to have made you *this* jaded."

A deep sigh rolled from my lungs, from my frustrated inner being, before I bent to rest my head on top of hers. "No one. And I'm not jaded. I'm reserved."

"Semantics," Flora breathed out, still pressed against me.

"What's this bouquet for?" I squeezed Flora's shoulder before moving to the wintry mix of flowers and accents.

"Mayor Tibbs asked me to make arrangements for the solstice ball." Flora clapped her hands together excitedly. "Leonard asked me to go."

"Leonard?" I blanched. "The faun?"

Flora scrunched her nose and threw her hands to her hips. "What's wrong with fauns? It's nice we're the same height. He doesn't have to touch his toes practically to kiss me on the cheek."

Giving a one-shoulder shrug, I sprinkled my magic over the flowers, giving them a sparkling, icy glow. "I always thought that was cute to watch them work for it."

Flora did her infamous giggle snort and admired my magical handiwork. "You *would* say that. Are you going? To the ball, I mean?"

"No, I don't—"

"Of course, she is," Jack's voice interrupted.

Flora and I froze, slowly turning on our heels to Jack standing in the doorway with his hands in his pockets. He wore his V-neck shirt and jeans, which were just as attractive as his finer attire.

"Wow. I didn't hear him coming through the door," Flora mused, whispering it to me like he wouldn't still hear.

"Neither did I. What did you do? Sneak through a crack as

a snowy backdraft?" I found myself tossing my hair from my chest as if I wanted to display my breasts for him. When his gaze dropped to them, I quickly pulled some hair back.

"Something like that. I can't reveal all my secrets straight away. A king has to have a few surprises up his sleeve, after all." Jack planted his most charming smile, his eyes focused solely on me, reeling me in with those ethereal sky-blue eyes.

Flora mouthed the word "king" to me, her eyes sparkling. I widened my eyes at her as a warning.

Flora giggled and playfully punched my arm. "You're taking Sylvie to the ball then, Jack?"

"That is—" Jack strode in front of me, his eyes searching my hair, a warm smile gracing his lips when he noticed my ears poking out. "—if she'll have me."

Have me.

My knees buckled. I cleared my throat, reaching for the counter behind me to steady myself.

"She says yes," Flora answered for me.

That brought me back to reality at lightning-fast speed, and I tossed her a seething glare.

"Perfect." Jack leaned forward, pressing his hand on the counter near my hip and making the muscle under that sleeve tattoo tense. "Will you let me give you a dress for the occasion, or are you going to be stubborn about that, too?"

I wanted to slap him as much as I wanted to laugh and suck his freaking face at such a snarky comment. Instead, my jaw dropped and I stood, bringing us a breath apart.

Flora appeared at our sides, and I could see her wide grin out of the corner of my eye.

"You know what? Alright, fine. Sure, I'll take the dress, Jack." Flashing him a coy smile, I lifted my chin, trying desperately to mask the way his scent was casting waves of pleasure in my core. His *scent*.

"Really?" Jack arched a thick blonde brow.

"Yup. I love dresses. And I also love the price of free. Win-win for me." I puffed out my chest because I had so won that.

A hearty laugh exploded from the depths of Jack's stomach, his eyes sparkling with mirth. "Fair enough. When's the ball?"

"Tomorrow night," Flora answered, still staring at us from the counter, sitting on it, and kicking her feet.

Jack and I never looked away from each other.

"And the time?" Jack asked.

I suddenly became acutely aware of the breath going in and out of our mouths—air shared between us from how close we were. Without realizing it, I used a single finger to search for his, grazing our skin together. I bit the inside of my bottom lip at how delicious it felt. The slightest touch had that blanketed coldness wrapping around me. Jack's eyes lazily panned to my finger, stealing the chill from him, and he curled his pinky with mine.

"Seven," Flora answered again.

Jack breathed out a subtle masculine purr. "Seven it is then. I'll meet you there." He pulled away from me just like all the times I had pulled away from him, denying me the euphoria I yearned to feel.

How could I blame him?

Flora blinked as she watched Jack heading for the exit. "What about the dress?"

While walking backward, Jack pressed a finger to the side of his nose. A shimmering pearlescent box appeared on the counter between me and Flora, sending our hair in plumes from the magic.

"I'll see you tomorrow, faerie," Jack said, bumping his ass into the door and disappearing into the snowfall.

Staring out the shop windows, hoping to see Jack within the shimmers of white still, I trailed my fingers down my throat and rubbed at the dip between my collarbones.

"Sylvie," Flora beckoned, tugging on my elbow and pointing at the beautiful box. "The box *itself* is pretty. Can you imagine what the dress will look like?"

Gulping, I moved in front of it, and we studied the box for a solid three minutes as if we were disarming a ticking bomb. "Should I open it?"

Flora smacked her hands on the table. "Of course, you should open it. At least get a sneak peek?"

Flora's raven, Dahlia, perched on the table beside us, cawing at the mysterious box.

Gripping the box's edges, I slowly lifted the top and gasped at the shimmering crystals lining the bodice. The dress was snow white with pale blue accents in overlapping shapes that appeared like snowflakes, wintry twigs, and a filigree-like design I had never seen. I traced my hand over it, my magic pulsing from my fingertips and showering the dress with sparkling silver and blue dust.

"Shit, I didn't mean to—" Rubbing my lips together, I tried to pull the magic back, but it didn't relent, content with interweaving itself into the dress's fabric and accentuating the already vibrant crystals and gemstones.

"I'd say, between the two of you, that dress is now fit for a winter *queen*," Flora said with a girly squeal, her wings fluttering enough to make her levitate from the ground.

It *was* beautiful. I'd never seen my magic react that way. I'd always been in complete control of it since the incident, and this was the first time that it responded to my emotions again, disregarding my shield.

If Jack and I really were mates, if what he said was true, that he could help control my power and use it to the utmost of my ability—what *could* I do?

Thirteen

Jack

I immediately trekked to Finneas' to talk to someone other than a polar bear and frost giant. I'd become far too much of a recluse in my older years, and I wasn't standing for it any longer. What did I intend to say to Finneas? What did I plan to ask? I hadn't a clue, but even sitting in silence surrounded by magical beings seemed better than sitting alone with my ass in the snow.

Wincing from the stifling heat as soon as I entered, I did my best to ignore it this time and slid onto a barstool. Decorations adorned the pub now: holly and evergreen garland, shimmering crescent moons, and bright sun ornaments.

Finneas noticed straight away, his bovine-like ears flicking upward in delight. "Well, well, hey, Jack. No offense, but you look like shit."

It hadn't dawned on me how incredibly exhausted I was until Finneas mentioned it. There was so much riding on my shoulders, and it somehow felt out of my hands. Other kings may have been so cruel as to force a claiming when they'd found their mates, to ensure their title and kingdom were sound, no matter how she'd felt about it. I wasn't that kind of king. If Sylvie didn't want me, didn't want what I could offer, then my kingdom would fall to Diedre. That thought weighed heavier because it meant my people would also be under her rule.

I stuck a thumb between my eyes and rubbed it frustratingly hard there. "I'm going to gather you are familiar with the concept of mates, Finn?"

"Of course. As far as I know, every magical species here has them in one form or another." Finneas blinked his large, orb-like, caramel eyes. "Sylvie. She's your mate."

"Yup," I replied, walking my fingers on the bar top, creating frosty designs as I went.

Two tumblers appeared in front of me, one with a whiskey double and one filled to the brim with ice. Scratching my cheek, I took the whiskey in my hand and held it out to Finneas. "Thanks."

"Going to take a wild guess and say it's not going as planned?"

I guzzled half of the liquor and stared at its amber-colored liquid. There wasn't a time I could recall where I felt this unsure about anything. Then again, I've never been in an actual relationship either. Women came and went, flings, and hook-ups to satisfy an itch that never fully got scratched from how uncomfortable it always was for me—the heat radiating from females. It left me feeling like my insides were melting, sweating profusely, and oftentimes made my vision blur. Another element Sylvie and I had in common for opposite reasons.

"It's not going badly, but it's also not going great. She's scared. I get it."

The bell chimed from the entrance door, and I whipped my head, deliriously hoping it would be a certain winter faerie with amethyst eyes. It was far worse—Thor. Growling, the possessive urges wrenching my spine, I gripped my glass with two hands. Thor spotted me and held up his palms, pointing to a corner table where he planned to sit *alone*.

Fucking thunderous asshole.

Turning back around, I received a disapproving brow arch from the minotaur bartender, the golden ring attached to his nose bouncing when he huffed. "You going to freeze the place again?"

"No, no. And about that, I—" The magical binging sound went off in my head, and I almost cracked the glass from my death grip on it. "—sorry, I need to take this."

"Take what?" Finneas asked, looking around.

Sighing, I downed the rest of the drink and slid a gold coin to him. "It's hard to explain. Trust me. I'll be back if I don't feel like plunging headfirst into a frozen lake after this."

Finneas chuckled and took the coin. "Sylvie will warm up to you, Jack. You'll see."

I certainly hope so.

Once outside, I flicked my hand in front of me, grimacing at the sight of Diedre. "What now?"

"Heavens, you could at least pretend like you're happy to see me every once in a while." Diedre used her middle finger to slather crimson color on her lips.

"Why in the *shit* would I do that?"

Diedre blanched as if my words offended her fragile ears. "There's no need for cursing like a barbarian, darling. I'm simply checking in. Glad to see you're faring no better than last time we spoke." The satisfied, smug grin she displayed had my blood freezing.

"What makes you say that?" I found a tree to lean on away from the town's center and crossed my arms.

90

"She's certainly not with you, and you look like someone turned your polar bear into a fur coat and mittens." Diedre ran her fingers over the arctic fox shawl she wore, a wicked glint in her eye that made me incredibly uneasy.

If she ever laid a finger on Nanok, I'd boil her alive.

"Nah, just a bit tired. Everything is going according to plan." I brushed snowflakes from my shoulder and stood taller.

"Oh? Does she know about your *true* form yet?"

My entire body tensed at that. It wasn't something that had crossed my mind. I'd rarely shown my ice creature form because there was never a reason for it. To claim her, however—I shot Diedre a glare.

Diedre cackled and bit her knuckle. "I'm going to take that as a no; oh, this is *rich*."

"Are we done here? I have better things to do than listen to your babbling. I know what you're trying to do, and it's not going to work on me." I moved closer to the mirage, pointing a finger at her and making the glacial eyes of my creature flash at her.

"You don't think for a second she'll be disgusted by that form? That she'll want to actually *fuck* it, Jakzair?" Diedre sneered at me and feigned gagging. "I certainly wouldn't."

"My creature would vomit at the thought of fucking *you*, I could tell you that much." The fury built in my chest, ice forming at my fingertips, and my limbs shook the more I held back.

She ignored my insult and leaned forward. "Just some food for thought, darling."

The mirage disappeared as ice daggers launched from my hands, lodging into a tree's trunk. My chest heaved, lungs burning, and I saw godsdamned stars. Diedre had always been a master manipulator, and her words never worked on me, never got under my skin—until now. If Sylvie could reject me as Jack, then she'd most certainly reject the *creature*.

Fourteen

Sylvie

A techno and violin version of *The Nutcracker* suite blared from the bakery speakers as I got to work on the tenth batch of sugar plums that Mayor Tibbs ordered for the town's winter ball tonight. An event I couldn't have forgotten about, even if I'd tried, with the dress Jack gave me, sitting in its ornate box on the back counter. Surely, we'd dance, which meant proximity. We'd be in each other's breathing space again, and his scent would be unavoidable. I've never paid attention to the way a male smelled quite as much as I did with Jack, and it never failed to make my core pleasurably *tighten*.

"Hello?" A familiar feminine voice shouted from the lobby.

Had I forgotten to put away the "chime for service" sign and lock the door? I really was distracted.

Wiping my hands on a towel, I sprinted to the front room, fidgeting with my phone to pause the music. Chelsea stood there with her arms folded, a bright smile playing over her lips, and her emerald eyes, with tiny crescent moons reflecting in them, beamed at me. "I take it you were supposed to be closed today on account of the big ball?"

"Yes," I replied through a deep sigh, shimmying past her to flip the sign and secure the dead bolt. "But now that you're here, what's up?"

Chelsea had really come into her own since moving to Arcane Cove without any knowledge of who and what lived here—one of three witches who called the Cove home. She fiddled with the pentagram charm on her necklace. "Dion's busy prepping for the afterparty in Bacchus, so I thought I'd sneak over and bribe you for a treat."

Dion, also known as Dionysus, Chelsea's mate, and god of wine, frenzy, and partying.

Chelsea's sweet tooth was the exact way we met when I found her in my bakery with her nose pressed to the display case. I'd sprinkled courage and relaxation magic over a vanilla cupcake with blue frosting that day, and we've since become good friends.

"No scandalous bribing needed, you know that." Grinning, I fished a plate of snickerdoodle cookies from the back of the case and rested them between us. "I was going to throw these away later tonight anyway. Help yourself."

Chelsea's eyes sparkled, and she grabbed two cookies. "You're a faerie *goddess*, Sylv."

Her compliment made my wings flap excitedly. I rubbed the tip of my ear with a sheepish smile. "Are you two attending the ball or is Dion too *cool* for it?"

"I'm going," Chelsea answered through mouthfuls of cinnamon and sugar dough. "Which means *he's* going. You?"

"Mmhm," I responded quietly, hopping on one foot and turning. "Better check on those nuts toasting for the sugar plums."

"Sylvie," Chelsea beckoned, following me when I didn't answer and soon matching my speed.

Doing my best to ignore her curiosity, I slipped on mitts and yanked the trays from the oven.

"Sylvie, you can't expect me to ignore the fact that you said you're going to the ball. Who's taking you?" Chelsea brushed crumbs from her hands and tossed her auburn hair over one shoulder, blocking me from moving any further once the trays were on the counter.

"His name is Jack. You might've seen him around town. Tall, spiky, snow-white hair and beard—" I trailed off, having to pinch my thighs together after envisioning his handsome face.

"Wait, yeah. The one with the ridiculously glacial blue eyes?" Chelsea pointed at her own emerald gaze.

Grabbing the food processor, I threw the cooled ingredients into it. "That's the one."

Chelsea nodded before realization washed over her, and she stood tall. "Sylv, is he—"

"Possibly," I whispered, staring at the sticky spots on my counter that I had yet to wipe off.

"Wait, but that's gr—" Chelsea started to say, her grin dropping into a smirk, her posture shifting so that one hip jutted to the side, her gaze becoming increasingly smug. "That's great if you want to deal with all of that *business*."

Chelsea's voice had gone an octave deeper than her normal pitch. It made my neck numb, so I removed my hands from the processor and pressed my palms to the table. "Business? What do you mean?"

Chelsea rubbed her middle finger over her lips, a peculiar glint flashing in her eyes. "He's a king looking for a queen, darling. A pretty thing to show off to the general public and nothing more."

Nausea bubbled in my stomach now. I pressed the button on

the processor to drown her out. I didn't like where she was going with this, and the glare I tossed her, along with my flared wings, should have told her as much.

With a sly grin, Chelsea reached over the counter and slapped her hand on the power button, dousing the noise. "I know you don't want to hear it, but I'm only saying it to protect you, Sylvie. He needs a queen for full reign, some pretty arm candy, and of course—" Her eyes panned to my stomach before launching back up. "—heirs."

As if I already had a tiny, pointy-eared being growing inside me, I pressed my hands over my abdomen, my throat constricting. "You act like you know him, Chelsea. You've never even met him. Maybe he wants someone to rule at his side, to *share* the burdens."

I'd haughtily spoken the words to Chelsea, but soon realized I needed to hear them myself, too.

Chelsea cackled and flicked an almond shell from the counter onto the floor. "Please. What man in history has ever wanted to share his power with their queen?"

Frowning, both my ears and wings folding back, I tore the lid from the processor and started scooping out enough to make frustrated balls of sugar plum fury. "What about Dion? He was different."

Chelsea dragged a finger down her sternum, lazily playing it over the dip between her breasts. "You're right. He *is* different. He'd want nothing to do with being royalty because he's too much of a free spirit."

Glancing at the shiny, silver box where the dress rested inside, her words ate at me like fermenting sugar. Something *pretty*. "You make it sound like he had a choice."

Chelsea slammed her fist onto the counter, making me jump

and drop the sugar plum I'd been rolling. "He *always* has a choice."

"Chelsea, are you okay? You're really starting to scare me." I slid the tray of sugar plums away from her and onto the counter behind me to save the rest of the batch from the other's fated floor drop.

Chelsea blinked and smoothed out her shirt. "What? I'm fine." Her demeanor softened, and she looked around. "Where are those cookies?"

Eyeing her peculiarly, I pointed to the lobby. "Where we left them. Next to the cash register."

"Right." Chelsea flashed a charming smile. "Tonight will be fun, huh?"

She walked away as if she hadn't just said several things to rock my already chaotically spiraling world. It made me wonder if her moon magic were trying to tell me something, speaking through her to say the things she'd never want to say for fear of hurting me.

Walking to the box, I opened it and ran my fingers over the jewels and beading, staring in delight at my magic pulsing through it. I'd wear the dress, I'd wait for Jack, and tonight—we were going to make several things as clear as freshly frozen water.

Fifteen

Jack

I'd been putting off showing Sylvie the ice creature because we had barely begun to be civil to one another. Revealing that she'd be expected to deal with a monster for the rest of her life. It lay dormant inside me, save for times of distress such as a heated battle that we couldn't have won without it, or—when I found my mate. I hadn't recognized the sensation at first, the icy tendrils chilling beneath my skin like pulsing wintry veins. The transformation was instant when I called on it in war, but this was entirely different. It felt like a godsdamned hard-on that I couldn't suppress or ignore if I *tried*.

Opting for attire I wouldn't normally wear to a ball for fear it would be overkill, I slid on the high-collared jacket, its length draping past my knees. It was patterned sapphire and silver embroidered filigree on the forearms, the white, curved lapels, and flared shoulder pieces. I stared at myself in the mirror as I did up the shiny silver buttons of the satin blue vest, a matching shirt underneath it, undone enough to expose my chest. Making the snowflake emblem of my kingdom appear in my palm, I positioned it at my waist's center, covering it with magic to make it sparkle and shine.

There was no telling how tonight would go. I'd be lying if I said I didn't fear her *not* showing up. It was an opportunity, however, to show her a side of me that I was far more confident with—my charm.

After settling into a pair of knee-high black boots, I patted the frost giant's enormous knee. "Thanks for letting me borrow your cave."

"You made it after all. I am curious as to why you did not use one of these so-called friends you claim to be making in the village's home, though." The frost giant sat on the stony ground, his back pressed to the cave wall, one knee hitched to his chest.

Chuckling, I took one final glance in the mirror, spearing a hand through my hair to make the waves perfect and slicking back the shaved parts above my ears. "It's winter. They all have raging fires or furnaces. I didn't want to sweat out my suit before I even set foot into the place."

"Heat around every corner. Sounds terrifying." A deep rumble vibrated from the giant's gut, his shoulders bouncing as if he'd learned how to laugh.

"You have no idea." Turning to face him, I splayed my arms at my sides. "How do I look?"

The giant shrugged. "Like a buffoon, but I still do not see the point in clothes."

Honestly? Neither had I. The world was far more comfortable without the restrictions of clothing, but I also couldn't recall many places where nudity was acceptable in public.

"I'll be seeing you," I said through a smile, exiting the cave to the awaiting snowfall. Pausing to let some of it coat my face, breathing the chill into my lungs, I use my magic to prevent snowflakes from settling on my head or clothes.

Nanok's head bumped under my arm, demanding a good scratching before I abandoned him for the night. Working my fingers over his head, ears, and chin, I pressed my palms to each side of his massive cranium. "Wish me luck, old friend."

Nanok responded by using his gargantuan, bluish-black tongue to slather my cheek with a slobbering kiss.

Wincing, I dragged the back of my hand over my face, ridding it of bear saliva, and patted his head. "Thanks."

It was already half past seven, and I'd purposely waited to avoid looking too antsy. Creating my icy rink trail, I calmly skated through the woods, resorting to a regular walking stance once I reached the plaza. Several other townsfolk were also arriving, and wearing elaborate gowns and tuxedos. They also wore some form of a *mask*—an important detail left out of my impromptu invitation.

Improvising on the fly, I called on the ice surging through the veins surrounding my eyes, allowing the creature to poke through there and only there—for now. It worked its way under my eyes, to my temples, over my nose, and covered my entire forehead. Once satisfied that the monster wouldn't try to take over more than what I was allowing, I moved for the door, holding it open for a female with light purple skin. Her crimson eyes flashed through her onyx mask as she walked past me, fangs glistening from the moonlight when she smiled. Offering a neutral grin in return, I ignored her frown and let the door shut behind me.

It took only a single moment to spot her through the crowd. My lungs forgot how to breathe, my heart refusing to beat as

I gawked at how absolutely fucking radiant she looked. The snow-white dress I created hugged her every curve, and the filigree branch designs with rhinestones and captured snowflakes sparkled from the candelabras. Her hair was more voluminous, with wisps of silver and blue to match the tint at the ends. She wore no mask, but silver stardust spattered her cheeks, her wings and ears on full display.

Sixteen

Sylvie

"After all of this, he's not going to show. I can't believe I actually put this dress on and have been looking at the door for the past half an hour like an idiot," I huffed, dipping a cup into the gigantic glass punch bowl filled with some form of tropical punch laced with ambrosia wine thanks to Dionysus.

"You're overreacting," Aella said in a sing-song tone. She wore a flowy blue dress with torn sections that mimicked water, leaving trails of silver glitter wherever she walked.

"Maybe. But I was already on edge about him. The least he could do is show up on time." Grumbling, I watched Chelsea and Dion dancing. She looked beautiful in her wine-colored sheath dress, Dion wearing a shirt to match, his usual torn jeans, and combat boots. Chelsea hooked a finger around one of his curved horns and brought his lips to hers, kissing him. I sighed and turned away, filling my glass with more punch.

"Maybe he's making himself look extra hot for you. *You* weren't even on time, Sylvie. Remember? All fussing over your hair? Wanting it more poofy?" Aella mimicked my bodacious, voluminous hair by raising her hands above her head.

A group of males, two demons, and a gargoyle chatted in a corner. One demon groaned and flicked his spade tail at the wintry surroundings.

"This place is lame. I heard they opened a burlesque on the outskirts of town. We should go check it out," said the antsy demon.

The gargoyle sighed and clicked his talons together. "Whatever."

"When you say burlesque, are we talking *all* females?" The other demon asked, appearing unamused at first.

"Nope," the other demon countered, crossing his arms. "Place is advertised as *anything* goes."

"I'm in," the suspicious demon said, all smiles now.

Growling, the gargoyle pointed between them. "Fine. But if you two get drunk off your asses this time, I'm not flying you both home. It's embarrassing how much you flail around and *sing*. Do we understand each other?"

The band leader demon slid an arm around the gargoyle's shoulders. "Of course, Vorthak. If we drink too much, we'll call for a Port-me-There, right Daevas?"

The other demon held up a pinky. "I'll pinky swear on it. Come on, Vorth, make use of your night off."

The gargoyle rolled his eyes and shoved Daevas's hand away before storming for the exit, the two demons in tow.

Mayor Tibbs approached us, his glowing, amber, reptilian eyes glancing around the elaborately decorated space. I'd hardly taken a moment to appreciate it, being so preoccupied with a certain Frosty the No-show Man.

Tibbs was a dragon who often donned his more human form, considering he'd scarcely fit anywhere in full form. The townspeople had elected him as head protector of the Cove long before I arrived. Tibbs scratched his head between two vertically curved black horns, the smaller version of his brown dragon wings folded behind him, the talons on the arches twitching as they moved. "I don't believe Town Hall has ever looked as festive. You all really outdid yourselves."

I popped a sugarplum into my mouth with an extra dose of pride. "Thank you, mayor."

Tibbs' copper, scaled tail whipped back and forth, dusting the floor, escaping through a custom hole in the back of his pants. Several females whispered, giggled, and pointed at Tibbs' handsome features, his long chestnut hair falling in waves to his chin.

"He's the only reason I ever attend town meetings," one female said, biting her thumbnail.

If Tibbs heard them, he paid it no mind, ever the professional. He lifted a pewter goblet to his lips, his hands matching the scaled texture of his tail, fingernails replaced with deadly black talons. "Have fun tonight, ladies."

"Tiberius, you old dog. Get your ass over here," Finneas yelled, waving the dragon mayor over, his long horns vibrating as he laughed.

Though his visit was brief, it was more interaction than I'd had with him in months. He always kept himself busy and obsessed over the Cove's safety. As he sauntered away, I noticed for the first time that he didn't wear shoes, his scaled, taloned feet clicking on the floor as he moved. My fascination with his reptilian form soon came to an abrupt halt. *Jack.* His calming scent, faint from this distance, hung in the air, and I closed my eyes, inhaling greedily.

"Sylvie? Is something—" Aella started, but cut her words short when she caught sight of Jack. "—Have fun." She leaned in to kiss my cheek, and I dragged my fingertips there, still staring through the crowd of Cove residents at Jack's resplendent choice of attire.

Jack's eyes met mine for a moment before a smirk played on his lips and he disappeared within the crowd. Blinking, as if I'd somehow imagined him, I turned circles, hitching my skirts to keep from tripping on them. My movements had become far too erratic, and I smoothed a hand down my bodice. My wings hadn't gotten the memo and continued to flap excitedly.

Townsfolk laughed, chatted, and danced circles around me, some accidentally bumping into my shoulders from my lack of attention. Nerves bubbled in my stomach, and I rubbed the tip of my ear, pulling some of my hair over it.

"Sylvie," Jack said, but he sounded far away. A hand delicately wrapped around mine and guided it away from my ear, leaving it exposed.

There was a flash of Jack's face, the same devious grin dancing on his lips, but Finneas's giant minotaur head soon blocked my view. Gasping, I shimmied past Finneas, ignoring his grumbles and mutterings of what was wrong with me. But Jack had already disappeared again. Was this his magic? Was he even *here*?

It had become an ethereal game of jacks, and *I* was the bouncing ball.

Jack's mocking chuckles echoed off the walls, and I stood still in the middle of the dance floor, frustration cinching my spine. "Are you looking for me, faerie? Got worried I stood you up, did you?"

Glaring into the void, I forced my wings to settle, only flapping languidly now. "Don't flatter yourself."

A male basilisk in a dark blue tuxedo, dancing with a female demon, gawked at me warily, a film flashing over his large, black orb-like eyes.

"Not you." Wincing, I lifted my hands. "Not to say you shouldn't be flattered by—"

Chilled lips pressed to the shell of my ear, scents of fresh snow and vanilla sending a furious blizzard swirling through my stomach. "How sweet," Jack said, his voice a low rumble that enticed a tightening in the depths of my core.

Chelsea's words about his true desires for a queen and my own determination to get the truth out of him catapulted me into whirling around to face him. I opened my mouth to speak, to yell, to demand answers, pushing away from him. Jack's hand snatched my wrist and pulled me toward him, my chest colliding against his ribs.

His actions were so brazen and abrupt that the words got lost in my throat. "What are you—" The mask Jack wore took my breath away. Not only was it entirely carved from ice, but it emerged from his skin like *bone*. It was a form of macabre beauty I never knew I could appreciate so fondly.

"I've come to realize that I've been going about this entirely the wrong way." Jack rolled his shoulders, drawing my attention to the satin shoulder pieces flaring from his jacket, the snowy white lapels with glittering silver filigree.

I wanted to run my fingers over the embroidery and even went so far as to lift my hand, but curled it away. "Oh?"

"Mmhm," Jack responded in a gravelly growl. "I believe my approach in persuading you needs to be a bit more—" Jack leaned forward, his bottom lip ever so slightly brushing the tip of my ear. "—tactile."

A pulse between my legs had me clenching my thighs together, his feathered touch on the point of my ear more sensual than I could've imagined. "What does that—"

Jack pulled me tighter against him, one hand trailing to my lower back, the other slipping into mine in an invitation to dance.

There were two sides to me now—the one that wished to throw all caution to the wind and give in to this, and the other that warned to seek out his intentions first. "If you think man-handling me is going to coerce me one way or the other, Jack, you've got another thing coming."

Jack trailed a finger up my back, sending delicious chilled magic through my skin with each vertebra he passed. "You haven't *begun* to feel the way I could handle you, Sylvie. What's your name, anyway? I imagine that's short for something?"

We slowly began to dance around the sea of townsfolk, a wintry waltz now playing over the speakers—a mix of violin, sleigh bells, and fantasy.

"Is it really that important to you?" I couldn't help roaming Jack's face, the chiseled bone structure, the well-kept beard—he was just so unbelievably handsome.

"Ah," he responded, moving his hand across my back, a knuckle grazing the bottom of one wing.

The brief touch made my breath catch in my throat, and I tensed—not because it hurt or because I didn't welcome it, but because it felt *nice*.

Jack's brow bobbed at my reaction as if he was storing that for later. "You feel like revealing such a secretive thing as your real name will put you at a disadvantage, I see." Jack picked up the tempo, flawlessly cascading us around the space without brushing another couple. "Let me take away that burden for you, then. My name is Jakzair."

His reveal had my mind humming, and a small smile edged my lips. "Just Jakzair? Not Jakzair Frost?"

Jack teased the callused tip of his middle finger against my palm and pressed his cheek to mine, his lips hovering by my ear. "Just Jakzair. Just Jack."

Without thinking, I nuzzled against him. "Sylvaria," I whispered.

Jack's grip tightened at my back, and a low growl bubbled in the back of his throat. "Did you happen to notice I designed this dress to accommodate your wings?"

Suddenly beginning to enjoy this game we were playing, I fluttered those same wings and leaned back to catch his gaze. "How thoughtful. Was it not also to have easier access to *other* parts of me?"

Jack's smile turned wicked, and he dipped a finger into the seam of my dress, his skin grazing my ass beneath the fabric. "Guilty. And you look—" Jack chewed on his bottom lip, his eyes scanning the bodice, the full tulle skirt, and the magic I'd sprinkled onto the fabric. "—like winter's radiance."

It was like a fairytale—the setting, the music, everyone dressed to the nines with masks, and the laughter surrounding us. As magical as we both were, though, the reality of it was anything but fantastical. Forcibly dragging myself from the cloud I'd been floating on, I moved one of my hands to Jack's shoulder, the other curling under his chin.

His glacial eyes darkened, and he trailed his fingers up my raised arm until he found my wrist, grasping it. "I sense a serious question coming on?"

"Why do you need a queen, Jack?" I held my breath, afraid of

108

his answer because I wanted so badly for Chelsea to be *wrong*.

Jack's lip twitched. "You deserve an honest answer. I don't *need* a queen. This was never about that. I found *you*, Sylvie. My mate. Whether I had been a king or not, that still would've been the case."

My heart fluttered at that, but I forced its hopeless romantic impulses down. "And if I reject this?" The words stung to ask, a boulder weighing heavily on my chest.

Jack didn't answer straight away, his jaw tensing, and he curled me closer until his pelvis pressed lightly against my stomach. "Then I would go about my business as I had before without ever bothering to look again."

"I—" The idea of Jack going through an endless lifetime without any hope gutted my insides. But then, agitation scraped my bones. "Are you just saying this to lock me in, Jack?" I tried to pull away from him, but he held me steadfast.

"What?" Jack asked a bit haughtily. "My kind only gets a chance at *one* mate, faerie. But I'm in no way going to ask you to accept me out of fucking pity either. I *do* have some pride."

"I didn't mean it like that," I whispered, wrapping my arms around his neck and fidgeting with his collar.

"You did. And I have to say I like the fire." A sensual smile graced Jack's lips, and his gaze roamed my hair, my ears, and settled on my eyes. "The only variety I ever dare play with."

Biting the inside of my cheek, I couldn't wait to ask it any longer. "Are you doing this for heirs?"

Jack nearly choked on his spit and pressed a fist to his mouth, coughing into it. "Yeti's ass, Sylvie. You're just cutting straight to it, are you?"

"I think a female has the right to know if you intended to rent the use of her womb for breeding purposes." My wings fanned repeatedly at the mention of *breeding,* and I ground my teeth together in an attempt to calm them.

A deliciously deep chuckle escaped Jack's throat, and he unabashedly slid a hand to my ass, squeezing it. "Breeding doesn't have to involve offspring, faerie. It could simply be for—" He trailed his nose up my neck, nuzzled against my jaw, and grazed his lips over my cheek. "—fun."

My heart rate rivaled that of a speeding dog sled now, and my breathing was doing its best to catch up to it. "You didn't answer my question."

"No," he answered gruffly. "I'm not opposed to the idea of ever having them, but my reign is different. I don't need heirs to carry on my bloodline because you see, Sylvaria, winter *always* comes."

He could've been lying, but every magical, intuitive part of me couldn't convince me of it. Bursts of confidence, determination, and a raging hopefulness settled over him like dustings of snow.

"I believe you," I said, my words distant because where did we go from here?

"Good," Jack responded, cupping the back of my head, his thumb making circles on my cheek. "Now we can move on to the *better* parts of courtship." He brought his mouth closer to mine.

I closed my eyes.

This was it. Jack was going to kiss me, and there'd be no turning back from it.

A buttery, masculine chuckle floated from Jack, his minty breath puffing against my awaiting lips. When his mouth didn't press to mine, I fluttered my eyes open. He was grinning at me, his canines larger and sharper now.

"Sylvie, Sylvie," Jack teased, pressing his cheek to the side of my head. He spun us in circles, his fingers dipping further into the back of my dress and kneading the top of my ass. "You look a bit *flustered*."

Tightening my grip on Jack's hand, I cleared my throat. "Not at all. We've just been dancing a while."

Jack smiled against my ear, whispering. "Do you want me to slow everything down?"

His words, the tone in how he said them, and that chilly breath teasing my skin made me *moan*. "Then how would we spend our evening?" I peeled back, looking into his eyes at first before lazily letting my gaze drop to his lips.

Still grinning, Jack curled a hand over my hip and hurriedly backed me into a darkened corner. My shoulders delicately met with the wall. Jack's arm pressed above my head. I beamed at him, my hands clenching his lapels. A shiver washed over me, but not from his chill, from *anticipation*.

Dipping his head, he pressed his lips to mine, soft and slow at first, the tip of his tongue sliding over my mouth. Whimpering, I melted against him, moving my arms around his neck to keep me upright. I parted my lips, inviting him in, but to my surprise, he didn't take me up on it. His teasing smile grazed my skin, and after a final peck, he pulled away.

"Goodnight, Sylvaria." Jack traced his thumb around my mouth, smoothing out the lipstick we'd smudged.

With a satisfied smile, no doubt in reaction to my stupefied expression, my mouth gaping open, eyes wide, he retreated. I stood numb and motionless, watching as the dancing, twirling bodies swallowed him, and Jack disappeared into the chilly winter night.

Seventeen

Sylvaria is breathtaking. I wanted with every fiber of my soul to tell her those exact words with the same awe and vulnerability I felt, but now was the time to puff my chest and show her how proud a mate I could be to her. The sweet nothings and pillow talk could come later and for the rest of our celestial lives—if she'd have me.

I'd let the snowy currents take me and paused to gauge her reaction from the frosted windows outside town hall. Sylvie stood dumbfounded and alone in the middle of the dance floor, still searching for me as if I'd return. The confused anguish in her gaze carved an icicle into my chest. Winter's blessing knows I wanted to continue what we started, to deepen the kiss and coax her somewhere private to explore *more*. I needed her to want this—to go searching for me, asking for us to continue the mate-ship.

Her delicate fingers traced over her lips, and only when Aella approached her, shaking her shoulder, did Sylvie seem to come to her senses. She muttered something to Aella and took another glance around the room. When her gaze flickered to the windows,

I hid out of sight, the ice creature itching at my skin, yearning to show more of itself. I wasn't sure how much longer I could hold it back, it'd *never* felt this insistent.

After several more minutes had dragged on, and Sylvie stopped looking for me, I began to lose a tinge of hope. She chatted with Flora and Aella, even took a few moments to dance with them, gleefully laughing and singing. If it weren't for the occasional glances over her shoulder and some grins that appeared forced, I may have worried she'd forgotten me entirely.

The ice creature forced itself from my forearms, icy stone and glacial skin replacing them. Grimacing, I pushed off the building, making for the woods and preparing to seclude myself until it calmed down—*if* it calmed down. Nanok was there to greet me, his large black nose sniffing the air, searching behind me, and huffing when he didn't detect a certain someone.

"She isn't *here*, Nanok. And I don't need *you* reminding me of that." Wincing in pain from fighting the creature, I gripped my chest, willing my heart not to completely freeze over.

Nanok huffed again and shoved me with a massive paw, nearly toppling me over. Anger flooded me, and the sharp ice spires that protruded from my creature's forehead forced their way out. Pointing at my bear, I flashed him a seething glare. "Don't push me right now. Can't you see what's happening?"

Nanok whimpered and stepped back, but soon his large eyes brightened, and he sniffed the air emphatically. I stilled because I smelled it too—sugar and watermelon. Taking a deep breath, I pulled my sleeves farther down my arms to cover the icy patches of skin that I couldn't dismiss.

Sylvie traipsed through the snow, a cheery smile plastered to her beautiful face. One hand held the skirts of the elaborate dress I'd made for her, the other clutched something to her chest. Her wings flapped behind her, accelerating her steps, and once she reached me, she was out of breath, and her hair no longer had its teased volume. She'd kicked off her shoes, running barefoot with porcelain feet wiggling snow between her toes. If she were anything but what she was, her feet would be nearing frostbite.

"Hi," Sylvie blurted, gulping and trying to catch her breath. "I—oh, did you add to your mask?" She eyed the new spires that had inconveniently sprouted from my head.

Choosing to skirt around the question, I held out my hand for her to take. Once her skin slid against mine, that delicious warmth soothing me, I let out a contented sigh. "Why didn't you *fly* here?" A tiny smile crept to my lips.

"Tried," Sylvie breathed out, shuffling through the snow to get closer to me. "Fell a lot. I really need to practice."

Her violet eyes sparkled as the full moon lit the snow collecting on the tree branches. My creature, my cock, and my soul *yearned* for her.

Biting the inside of my cheek *hard* to tame the monster, I pulled her closer and pointed at what she hid in her hand. "What do you have there?"

"Oh," she said, her voice so delicate the harsh winds surrounding us almost carried it away. "You seemed a little down at the ball, and I get it. It's me—"

I opened my voice to protest, but Sylvie pulled her hand from mine and lightly pressed it over my mouth. Keeping my gaze locked with hers, I skimmed my tongue over her skin, slipping it between two of her fingers.

She hitched a breath, watching me, and gulped. "You were right, Jack. I am scared." Sylvie revealed what she'd been hiding—a white cupcake with blue and white frosting speckled with silver dust. "Which is why I made this for *both* of us to eat."

The ice creature rumbled in my chest. I lifted her hand from my lips, shifting my gaze between the delectable, magic-laced treat and the nerves dancing so obviously in her eyes. "You're *offering* me food?"

Sylvie blinked and re-emphasized the cupcake in her grasp. "Well, yes. You take a bite, I take a bite, and things should settle. It's a clarity spell."

She wasn't aware of the implications of being fed by your mate meant for our kind. Why would she? An internal battle on whether to make this known to her, or use it to my advantage to tether her, raged within me.

Closing the remaining distance between us, I wrapped a hand around her forearm. She was so delicate compared to me that I could've circled one of my hands around hers *twice*. Slowly, I brought the cupcake toward my lips, flashing a glint in my wintry eyes in hopes of keeping her captivated. A smile edged the closer the icing got to my mouth, and I opened it, my canines enlarging—anticipatory and feral.

The ground rumbled at our feet, snapping me and Nanok's attention straight to it. Sylvie backed away, the snowy dirt beginning to split apart. Harrowing cackles and chatters emanated from the hole before dozens of creatures wielding icy blades, rows of razor barbed teeth, and skin bulging with sharp icy spikes crawled from it.

Frost goblins.

Sylvie peered at me with terror, her eyes wide as the full moon hanging above us. The crack grew larger, separating us. Several goblins scurried toward her. She held the cupcake above her head, using her magic in spurts to keep them at bay.

When she looked at me, yelling an agonized, "Jack!", there was no more hiding the ice creature. It *erupted* from me.

Eighteen

Sylvie

If it weren't for Fintan bursting through the tree line to my aid, skewering several goblins with his antlers as they neared me, I might have taken several swords to the stomach. What Jack turned into—the gradual process as the icy armor climbed up his arms, torso, and head—had me staring in awe and fear, but mostly in *adoration*. Jack's skin turned a pale blue, layers of armored icy plating shifting over his chest and stomach. Several lethally sharp icy spikes protruded from his shoulders, down the sides of his arms, and continued the length of his forearms. He was much taller than me before the transformation, but now he *towered* over me. Jack's hair and beard were replaced with icy sculpture renditions of them, spiking on his head and pointing down his chin. Two larger spikes extended from his forehead like a horned helmet, and his eyes were glowing pools of cerulean.

Fintan slid in front of me, blocking my view of the beautiful monster Jack had become, and it snapped me back to what was happening. Dozens of small frost creatures ran chaotically around us, some tugging and tearing my dress skirts. Not only was the fear of them harming me running loose in my mind, but they were destroying my dress—such a simple garment, but a *treasure* that Jack had created for me.

The cupcake was still in my grasp, and I made it disappear into an invisible pocket created from the snowfall for safekeeping. Hiking my dress, I used my wings to launch myself skyward, landing on Fintan's back and grabbing onto the back of his neck for dear life.

Nanok raised on his hind legs, growling and baring his massive canines. The once docile polar bear raged with carnal fury, his eyes taking on the same icy glow as Jack's, as if they were connected somehow. While Nanok swatted leaping creatures, Jack created ice swords protruding from his forearms, slicing them in the air in front of him, dismembering all who crossed their paths, misting their dark blue blood.

As much as I'd love to admit that I knew what I was doing in a battle, I hadn't the first clue. Sending bursts of my magic to stagger them away was one thing, but how to wield a sword, or make those spur of the moment life defying decisions? Just because I was magical, just because I was fae, didn't mean I'd suddenly become a renowned fighter no sooner had a hilt graced my palm. I didn't feel ashamed that Fintan wasn't charging me through enemy lines to attack them, though I certainly bashed any available heads that wouldn't knock me off my stag. Fintan was protecting me, making it harder for them to attack or grab me as we tried to flee.

Nanok and Jack were watching each other's backs. Jack used his blades to take out those closest to him, others who were wise enough to try and flee back to the hole, he'd launch flying icy daggers at. They had so many in their backs by the time the creatures hit the ground, they looked like frosted porcupines. We reached a clearing with Jack distracting most of the horde.

Whirling Fintan around, I kept him steady despite his huffs and hoof scrapes, yearning to join in the fight. I needed his sharp antlers to ward off any that might have slipped past. A few of the creatures leapt to Jack's back, one accidentally catching his ear on a shoulder spike. He yelped, attempting to pry himself free, but Jack yanked him off only to shove his entire head through the spikes. The creature became a grotesque decoration dangling from Jack's shoulder while he fended off the rest. The sight of that, the experience of all of it, should've disgusted me more, but it simply *didn't*.

These things were clearly here to harm us, if not ordered to kill us. The instant Jack sensed trouble, sensed that I was in danger, he morphed into this other side of him that he had yet to mention. No doubt this beast of his was menacing, dangerous, and bordering on barbaric, and I'm sure he worried I would find it disturbing. No, I wanted to see it up close. I wanted to run my fingers over the dull sections of the icy spikes that were a part of his skin.

I'd become so distracted by the arctic force that was Jack Frost, I didn't see the creatures lurking behind us. Fintan kicked his back legs and swung his antlers, but there were too many of them for him to counter on his own. One jumped and latched onto my hair, dragging me from my stag and into the snow. Another pinned my wings to the ground, and I shrieked at how painful the pressure was—a pain I'd never experienced.

Jack roared as he stormed through the clearing, throwing creatures into tree trunks, their bones breaking and cracking, the sound amplified by thick forest. He stomped on several others, their small forms trapped under his gigantic, icy haunches. Jack impaled the creature who'd yanked me by my hair and the one that still had me pinned—he grabbed it by the head, turned away from me, and using only his hand, popped the creature's skull like a grape.

The creatures began to retreat after this, scurrying to the foggy hole. Nanok swiped at them as they passed, killing many more who dared to try to walk past him to the safety of the hole. When the last creature toppled into the opening in the ground, it sealed shut, and the only evidence that they were here at all was the hundreds of body parts and scattering mass of blue blood staining the snow.

Wincing, I sat up, my right wing still hurting. I frowned at the small tear in it, making the top curved portion bend.

Jack was still in his monstrous form, his head shaking, his hand beating against his skull like he was trying to morph out of it. Drool dripped from Nanok's jowls, and he stood in a combat stance, lips curling in a snarl.

"Jack," I eased, fanning my palms at him and rising. "They're gone now."

I had no idea what to expect from this side of him, but in my gut, in my heart, I knew even this version wouldn't hurt me.

"Was this not enough for you?" Jack roared, his voice far deeper, far more gravelly than his normal voice.

"Enough?"

Jack dragged one arm sword through the snow, bumping into arms and heads. "The carnage I displayed for you—to protect you. Is this not *enough* to prove what kind of mate I can be to you?"

My heart raced at how feral he sounded, and it nearly burst out of my chest when he began to pace in circles like a cornered wolf. I had to tread this one very, very carefully.

Not daring to move closer, I kept my hands out in front of me. "Jack, I appreciate you protecting me. Thank you for that. Times have changed, though; it can't just be some—"

Jack sheathed the ice swords into his arms, leaving only the spiked barbs at his wrists and elbows. He prowled toward me, and I shook uncontrollably, gulping once he stood in front of me. I had to lean backward to look him in the face. "You are *mine*, Sylvaria. You are my *mate*. I *own* you. It is that simple."

Not knowing where the sudden burst of confidence came from, I rolled my shoulders back and glared at him. "I'm not a possession, *Jakzair*. And this isn't you talking."

"That is where you are wrong. This is me in my truest form," the monster said, bowing forward to bring our faces closer.

The spikes, barbs, and sharpened bits of him were intimidating, but those eyes—Jack was *still* there, and I knew no matter how much he huffed and puffed, he wouldn't ever hurt me.

"No. This isn't your truest form. It's a part of you that you haven't needed in a long time."

Jack clenched his fists, his icy skin and armor cracking and misting. "Because of you. Because you are my mate. Because you are—"

Mine. The craziest part was that I loved hearing it and I wanted to be able to say Jack was mine, too.

"Jack, I'm going to walk away now. Because for the first time in your ethereal life, I think you need to *cool* down."

The beast blinked at me, and Nanok too grew more submissive, flopping onto his butt and tilting his head to one side.

Sucking in a deep breath, I reached forward and placed a hand over where Jack's heart would be. With my icy warmth pressed to his chest, steam wafted underneath my touch. "I appreciate you protecting me. Come find me when *Jack* is ready to talk."

Fintan came to my side and knelt for me to climb on his back. My stag blew a puff of air at Jack through his nostrils before he carried me into the forest. My shoulders shook from the fear I'd felt from daring to come toe to toe with such a creature, but it soon fizzled away because it wasn't just any monster. It was Jack, *my* winter monster king.

Nineteen

Sylvie

"You say gingerbread people and I say they still look like *dicks*," Tambie announced, waving her finger at my newly displayed tray of cookies in the case.

Aella pinched the bridge of her nose and pointed. "The arms are folded in, Tamb, see? They're holding the candy cane."

Tambie's black pixie cut hair swished around her face as she shook her head. "Nope, I see balls—" She gestured toward the legs with wide feet. "—and a bulbous crown." She circled the cookie's head.

Smiling, I wiped the counter and shrugged. "I don't have a problem calling them gingerbread dickheads."

"See? Now that's keen marketing." Tambie flicked one small, tan fawn antler at her temple and threw an arm around Aella's shoulders.

Tambie and Aella were two of several maenads who worked at the nightclub Bacchus and had forever been connected with Dionysus. These two maenads in particular, though, were the only ones I'd witnessed that seemed like true sisters.

Now that Tambie had pointed it out, I couldn't unsee how large I'd made the feet. Usually, my cutting and shaping skills were pristine, given the magical accompaniment, but then again, I *was* knee deep in distractions.

It had been two days since I left Jack in the woods with the ultimatum, only to look for me when he was ready to talk. It'd been agonizing to wait, but I promised myself I wouldn't be the first to go searching for him this time. Was he still stuck as his monster? Did he not appreciate how I left things, and now did not want anything to do with me? Today would be the third day, and the impatient gnat flying circles around my head was starting to become unbearable.

The bell over the door chimed, and I snapped my gaze to the entrance, inconveniently hoping it'd be a certain blonde frosty stud.

"Evenin', ladies," Herb the sheriff greeted, tipping his ten-gallon hat.

Clearing my throat to keep my obvious disappointment from showing, I forced a grin and waved. "How are you today, sheriff? It's been a while since you stopped by the bakery."

Herb laughed and patted his round belly. "While I love your treats, Sylvie, my gullet can't seem to handle them as often as it used to." His spurs sounded as he walked toward the counter, his gait wide, legs slightly bowed.

Herb was a porcupine shifter, which was partially apparent in his appearance—a broad, blunt nose with thin nostrils, and midnight black, glossy eyes beneath wrinkled eyelids.

"Something wrong, sheriff?" Tambie asked, frowning.

She had reason to be skeptical. If the sheriff wasn't arriving somewhere for a drink, food, or to strike up a conversation, it wasn't usually good news.

"Welp, something alarming was discovered in the woods this

morning. We're talking so far in that most folks wouldn't be able to get there on foot in these freezing temperatures." Herb rubbed a knuckle under his salt-and-pepper moustache which stretched to either side like quills.

Warily, I glanced at my feet that had made that trek effortlessly days ago.

"Oh, no," Aella said, sighing. "What'd you find, if I even want to ask?"

Herb tapped a hairy finger on the hilt of his six-shooter strapped at his side. "We ain't seen them around the Cove before, but I swear they were some forms of goblins. Dozens of them—dead in the snow."

Numbness coated my throat like hardening caramel, and I wrung the cloth in my hands.

"Goblins?" Tambie echoed. "In the Cove?"

"We figure it may have something to do with Sage's murder, seeing as that too was out of left field." Herb stared longingly at the treats in the display case.

Sage, the murdered pixie from months ago, was still not able to be figured out.

Without thinking, I blurted, "No. Couldn't be."

"I beg your pardon?" Herb's bushy brows rose, and he smacked his lips together. "How would you know that?"

Tambie and Aella shot me quizzical looks, their arms folded.

Jack had arrived in the Cove long before Sage's death, so that didn't match up, and Jack wasn't a killer unless prompted—unless he felt compelled to *protect*. I couldn't reveal any of this, however, because I didn't want him tied to anything, especially when it was about me.

Rubbing the tip of my ear, I puffed my chest. "Serial killers normally have repeated motives. The acts are usually similar. Sage was killed from the inside out, by poison or magic. How would you say the goblins were killed?"

I'd almost fucked that up by stating precisely how they were killed when the sheriff had yet to reveal that.

Herb squinted at me curiously, but obliged by answering, "Dismembered. Beheaded. They looked like damn shish kabobs."

Aella gagged, and Tambie patted her back, thoroughly intrigued by what Herb was saying.

Tapping my lip, I held out a hand to Herb. "Sounds like a blade of some kind. Opposite to Sage. How far have you gotten in that case, anyway?"

Deflection.

Herb shoved his hat up far enough to scratch his forehead. "I suppose you're right. And the evidence on Sage's case is about as empty as a bear's belly comin' out of winter slumber."

"That's a shame," Tambie said, her tone somber. She continued to rub Aella's back.

"Alright, ladies, I'm going to go ask some more folks if they saw anything in those woods. You take care now." Herb turned to leave.

"Sheriff," I beckoned, removing an apple fritter from the case. Quickly shimmering gold magic over it, I held it out to him. "One for the road? It's sugar-free."

And laced with affirmation. Here's hoping it convinced him thoroughly that the goblins had nothing to do with Sage.

"Sugar-free, you say?" Herb chuckled and hooked his thumbs in his suspenders before taking the fritter. "Don't mind if I do, then. Thank you kindly, Miss Sylvie."

"You're welcome." The smile curving my lips was genuine this time.

Once Herb left the shop, I blew out a breath. "Gals, I need to know more about mating."

Tambie coughed on her spit, and it was Aella's turn to slap her back. "Well, that was random."

"Not really," Aella countered.

"I've found my mate, and I was told I would never have one." I picked at a hangnail forming on my thumb. "I don't know the first thing about mates and don't want to be in the dark about this. He shouldn't be the only one in the know."

Tambie's eyes went wide, and she hopped. "We should talk to Dagnar."

"Why not the boss?" Aella unenthusiastically folded her arms. When Tambie didn't answer, she elbowed her in the ribs. "To Dion?"

Tambie slowly nodded, seemingly mulling over what Aella suggested. "We should talk to Dagnar," she said again, this time more gleefully and energetically.

"Alright, let's talk to the main orc man." I moved from behind the counter, but snapped my fingers at the setting sun. "Perfect timing. Aegean should be here any minute to take over the night shift."

Aegean was one of the merfolk, granted legs to walk on land at night so long as they were back in the water before the sun fully rose the following morning. When he'd applied to my ad for a second baker, I'd been skeptical at first, given he spent half his life underwater. Color me surprised when he'd flown through my kitchen as if it were his own and made three dozen cinnamon rolls. I hired him on the spot.

"I'll head over there and let him know we're coming. Considering the subject matter, I feel like a guy could use a heads up about such things." Tambie jutted her thumb in the direction of the café before hitch-stepping out the door, sprinting once she'd reached outside.

"I assume Tambie has a thing for Dagnar?" I couldn't help but grin.

"Yeah," Aella answered, sighing. "But he's tied to this damn succubus chick. Poor Tamb. Goddess bless her, though, she still seeks every opportunity to hang out with him as *friends*."

The bell chimed. Aegean waltzed in, slapping his hands together and already prepping to start the night's work. "I'm here to relieve you, Sylvie." Long, thin auburn hair fell to his hips, Aegean's striking topaz eyes brightening at the prospect of baking for the night. Golden scales shimmered at the corners of his jaw, down his neck, and continued over his shoulders, forearms, and hands.

"Thanks, Aegean. Right on time." Walking past him, I held out a set of keys and dropped them in his palm. "In case I'm not back in time, feel free to lock up. I have an extra set. I'd hate for you to miss your curfew."

Aegean took them but flashed me a sly grin. "Sure thing. You planning a nightcap?"

My core swooshed at the thought of spending a night with Jack. "We'll see."

Aella snort-laughed when we exited the bakery, playfully shoving my shoulder. "We'll see? You sultry *slut*."

Tambie was already chatting away with Dagnar at the bar when we arrived at The Minty Boar. Dagnar spotted us and held up a big green hand, waving us over. I curled my fingers through the ends of my hair, nervous but excited to have this conversation and finally know what to expect—how to deal with it all, and if I *wanted* to accept it.

Aella gave one of her cutesy emphatic waves before taking a seat on a stool.

"And speak of the angel," Dagnar said, motioning for me to sit.

Stretching my wings, wincing at the soreness still plaguing the right one, I moved them out of the way before sitting.

Aella gasped. "Sylvie, your wing. I hadn't noticed before." She frowned and moved her face closer to the injury.

"It's fine. Just a little tear. It'll heal up in no time." I gave a reassuring smile despite not knowing if it would, in fact, heal, but I had more pressing matters.

"Tambie tells me you found yourself a mate?" Dagnar's smile accentuated his two lower tusks.

Folding my hands on the bar top, I sat straighter. "It would appear that way. But I don't know the first thing about it because they never taught me."

"First," Dagnar started, turning to one of three golden taps lining the back wall. When he faced me again, he rested a tankard full of frothy ale in front of me. "You'll probably need this."

Tambie cleared her throat. "And what about us? We're her *support* group."

"Alright, alright," Dagnar replied, chuckling as he filled two more mugs. He leaned a forearm on the bar top and eyed me empathetically. "I need to warn you that I'll help the best I can, but it could be different for orcs compared to—" He used a black talon to scratch the back of his emerald head. "—what are they?"

How did I answer this? I didn't know *what* I saw in the forest that day.

"He's fae, but has this beast or monster he turns into—a wintry one." I raised my arms above my head to gesture how large he'd become in that form.

"Like the abominable snowman?" Aella asked, holding her mug with both hands and sipping from a straw.

Tambie leaned in closer. "That's hot."

Dagnar arched a thick, green brow at Tambie and then turned to me for confirmation.

"No, no. Not furry and growly. He's made entirely of ice with these spiky arm swords and spiky shoulder pieces." I stared at nothing as I did my best to articulate into words what I'd witnessed. "His beard, his hair, his muscles, they all turned into *ice*."

Tambie rested her chin on her hand. "That's even hotter."

Mimicking her action, I rested my cheek against my palm. "You're telling me."

"If he's got a monster form, no matter if he's permanently in it or not, like an orc or gargoyle, then I'm going to guess the rituals, if you will, are quite similar." Dagnar held up a claw, pausing when a customer ordered a meat pie.

"Are you nervous?" Aella asked, rubbing my shoulders.

"Yes," I whispered, my stomach catapulting into flurries of fireflies. "But I'm also excited at the prospect of something I never thought I'd be able to have."

Aella hugged me to her side, pressing her rosy apple cheek against my pale one.

"Sorry about that, gotta keep the hungry fed." Dagnar rubbed a hand over his apron-covered stomach. "Now then, the first step would be offering food. That lets the male know the female is interested enough to continue the process."

My heart fell to my feet.

The cupcake. I'd offered him the first bite. Was he going to let me start this without telling me the *implications*?

"You alright?" Tambie asked. "You look a little flushed."

There's no telling if Jack would've stopped it. The goblins ambushed us before he had a chance one way or the other. It was still something I'd put a giant pin into for later.

"I'm good. Please continue." I gestured to Dagnar.

Dagnar crossed his arms, making his already titanic muscles bulge. Tambie's gaze darted straight to them, and she covered her face with her mug, guzzling from it. "There'd be accepting it, which normally involves, um, *bedroom* time—"

"Sex," Aella countered. "He means hot, sweaty, carnal sex."

My stomach did a delicious dip, and I pinched my knees together.

Dagnar snickered and shook his head. "And the last part, the no turning back, clinching of it all—is the claiming. However, I'm not sure what his would entail, or yours. Every species is different."

Tambie swiveled on her stool, doing one complete turn. "Maenads scratch the fuck out of their back."

"Tambie, for goddess's sake, you make it sound so barbaric. One scratch would do it," Aella added, her cheeks turning crimson.

Letting them all converse, I busied myself with gulping several mouthfuls of ale.

"Says you, Aella. Me? I'd scratch the living shit out of my mate so that everyone knew—" Tambie lifted a small claw. "—that they are *mine*." She leveled her gaze on Dagnar.

Dagnar scratched one of his tusks, obviously intrigued but attempting to hide it.

"What if I don't know how my kind claims?" The sympathetic looks they all threw my way made me feel about the size of a field mouse.

"You'll know even if it's not until that precise moment. *Everyone* knows, Sylvie," Dagnar encouraged.

Tilting my head back, I finished my drink and wiped my arm over my mouth to rid it of foam. "I really appreciate all the insight, Dagnar, but I should probably try to get a little sleep before I have to relieve Aegean at the bakery."

"Or so you're energized for tons of mating sex," Tambie countered with a snort.

Aella hopped from her stool and hugged me. "Let me know if you need anything at all, okay? Even if it's watching the bakery."

"Thanks, Ael. And thanks again, Dagnar. Also, for the ale."

Dagnar bowed his head. "Any time."

I trudged to my cottage in a daze, repeating everything Dagnar told me and what transpired between us since Jack's arrival. I opened my door and eyed my awaiting bed, but didn't feel like crawling into it. Instead, I called on Fintan, and when he lay down and rested his head on his curled-up front legs, I nestled against him. With his warmth and my power, I wouldn't freeze, and I let slumber take me amidst the chill and snowfall.

Twenty

Jack

It took me days to calm the creature. The first twenty-four hours after Sylvie had so wisely left me alone in the woods, the beast refused to let me revert to my fae form. I spent hours wrestling with Nanok in an effort to work off some of the insatiable energy, but not even that satisfied it. It was when I refused to do a damn thing that the monster became more annoyed than restless. I used meditation techniques taught to me by the soothsayers in my kingdom, disconnecting the mind and focusing on the soul.

The creature still beat at my skull, trying to edge its way in, but I was far too gone to let it under my skin. It was now the morning of the fourth day, and the closest I was going to get, given there was little time left to convince Sylvie to be mine. I wanted nothing more than to claim her the moment she accepted it, but she'd trusted me enough to reveal she's never fully *been* with a male. The first time should be showing her what I could offer her in that sense for the rest of eternity—that she would be more than a queen to take up the emptiness on the throne next to me or some simple incubator for my would-be heirs.

I coaxed most of the beast away, but my icy hair and beard remained, as well as a border around my eyes. My magic still overtook my gaze as well, that same glowing blue hue radiating in my eyes.

"Does it look that bad? Think she'll accept me like this?" I asked Nanok, turning in a circle with my arms out at my sides.

Nanok raised his snout and made a chuffing sound, his form of a laugh.

Frowning at him, I shoved his shoulder and dragged a hand over the icy beard weighing heavily on my chin. "What would you know about attracting a female fae, anyway?"

My polar bear squared off his shoulders and bared his teeth as if when he were trying to impress a would-be mate.

"Fine. I know you're a handsome bear, Nanok. I swear, you're always fishing for damn compliments." Grinning sidelong at him, chuffing again, I turned my gaze to the skies.

The evening drew closer, and I knew it was about time for her to switch shifts with her assistant. With any luck and a whole lot of wishing on a winter's star, she'd go straight back to her cottage for the night. I couldn't wait any longer. My kingdom, my people, couldn't wait any longer. And I'd gone long enough without a mate, a companion, a lover. I wanted to make her my world, destroy anything that'd dare harm her, and show the entire winter kingdom why they, too, should cherish her the same way.

Hooves scraped the ground, putting me on alert, but those antlers put me at ease. I'd recognize those icy wonders anywhere—Fintan. As relieved as I was, it was him, not something attempting to attack us again. It also deflated me. If Fintan was out wandering the woods, it meant Sylvie wasn't home.

Fintan stood motionless for a beat, his jaw rotating as he

munched on berries that survived the frost. He moved closer and bumped his head against my arm.

"Hey now, buddy, what are you doing?" I dodged his sharp antlers from scraping my skin.

Fintan blew a puff of air through his nostrils before bumping into me again, this time harder and in a specific direction. His strength was enough to make me stumble forward. I gawked at where he wanted me to go—Sylvie's cottage. Letting Fintan lead the way, I willfully followed behind him, Nanok at my heels. When we stepped over the hill, Sylvie's home coming into view, a breath caught in my throat. She wasn't inside like I'd expected her to be, but sat at a frozen pond's edge, dressed in a snow-white dress, a lace overlay littered with snowflakes amassing the ground around her. Her head turned to look at me as if she could sense my presence, and those striking amethyst eyes blazed from the blanket of white surrounding her.

Fintan nudged me again. I waved him off, slipping my hands in my pockets as I made the rest of the way to her. I was barefoot, the same as she, and the sight pulled an emphatic grin to my lips.

"I'm sorry I didn't come to you sooner. You wanted Jack, and my creature is—" I scratched the back of my head. "—demanding as of late."

Sylvie rose, her eyes roaming the parts of the monster that remained. "I can see that."

"Have you—" Spotting the tear in Sylvie's wing, making a portion of it bend, I lurched forward. "Sylvie, your *wing*."

My brave mate shook her head and glanced behind her. "It's nothing."

"It causes you pain. That is *not* nothing, faerie," I countered, lifting my hand to it and stilling her with a firm grip on her shoulder when she startled. "I'd never hurt you." Willing my ice blue magic toward the tear, it healed in a spiral of snow until it appeared as if nothing had happened.

Sylvie gasped and flapped her newly repaired wings, a resplendent smile that I put there gracing her face. "Thank you. I didn't know you could do that."

"I can't do that for everyone." I recoiled my hand, resisting the urge to feel her skin. "Just—"

"Your mate," she finished for me, her eyes gleaming at the mention of that.

My heart throbbed in my chest with the ease with which she said it.

"Jack, I'm going to ask you one question, and I want you to be honest with me." Sylvie quirked a blonde brow, awaiting my agreement.

"Alright."

She stepped closer, dragging the lace train behind her. "When I offered you that cupcake. Were you going to take a bite of it before telling me it would be me accepting our bond?"

My blood froze, and I clenched and unclenched my hands several times. There was no point in lying about it. Either I lied and she saw through my bullshit, or I told her the truth and she'd forgive me or tell me to take a hike. Either way, I'd know.

"At first, no, I wasn't going to tell you because I wanted you tethered to me no matter what the cost."

Her throat bobbed, and a frown formed on those gorgeous, plump lips.

"But, right before the frost goblins attacked, I was riddled with guilt, and I wasn't going to take a bite." Risking it, I took Sylvie's hand in mine and brought it between us, pressing a chilled kiss to her knuckles. "And that's the truth."

Sylvie slowly nodded, her faerie magic surrounding us in shimmers of cerulean, silver, and white. She produced an identical cupcake to the one she'd offered the first time and held it up to me. "Then take a bite and join me for a soak." She edged her head past the pond where a small hot spring resided, surrounded by snow-covered moss and grey stones.

My chest squeezed, tightened, and the creature's carnal desires surged, knowing what this all meant. Keeping our gazes locked, I took a bite, blue frosting covering my lips and the tip of my nose. Sylvie stood on her toes and delicately slid her tongue over my lips, licking away the icing, followed by sucking the tip of my nose.

She backed away, working down the shoulders of her dress, displaying those perfect, porcelain breasts. The seduction waltzing in her eyes was like she'd done this act a hundred times over. The fact that this was new territory for her, however, *mesmerized* me.

Sylvie sauntered to the hot spring, letting the dress fall past her ass and onto the snowy bank before dipping a toe into it. She beckoned me with a single finger.

My mate may have never been entirely with a male, and may not have the experience to back her brazen display, but my creature growled at the sight of her naked form disappearing into the steamy water. As I followed her, I knew she was blossoming into a seductress because of *me*.

Twenty-One

Sylvie

There was no sound explanation as to how I'd found my inner vixen. All of Jack's forms were gorgeous—the fae, the man, the icy parts of his creature. The anticipation of what was to come, now that I had started it, had me in a tantalizing mix of excitement and trepidation. The warm water was a delicious embrace to my skin, the coldness of my magic reacting to it, creating floating ribbons of steam. I turned in time to see Jack naked, standing at the pool's entrance and *watching* me. My gaze unabashedly roamed his chiseled, muscled form, starting at the sleeve tattoo wrapping his right arm, the carved chest muscle, six-pack abs, and that thick, intimidating *cock*.

It appeared the same as the male I'd been with all those years ago, another fae, but Jack's glowed with bright blue veins that matched his eyes. I sank into the water up to my breasts, letting my nipples peek above the surface. Jack took calculated, slow steps into the spring, pressing his hands to each side of the stones surrounding me. He lowered his face to mine and kissed me— hard, deep, and with such ferocity I could tell he'd been holding it in for centuries as he claimed.

Wrapping my arms around his neck, my own impatience wearing thin, I kissed him back—feverishly, ravenously. With my touch, he could withstand the heat from the hot spring to enjoy its warmth. His icy beard pressed against my chin, cooling my face, while my legs remained warm from the pool. Jack curled an arm around my lower back and carried me to the edge, resting me on the snow-covered moss. Snowflakes fell around us in droves, collecting in my hair and eyelashes.

Jack lifted a finger, his magic surrounding it, turning it into shimmering ice. He dragged it between my breasts, the chilled sensation calling to me as a winter faerie, making my wings go taut. Jack moved to one nipple, flicking it, and making me moan before sliding his finger down my stomach. He paused above my clit, teasing me there, gliding back and forth before pressing against it. The intensity had me writhing, but Jack kept a hand at my back, steadying me. When he moved his finger lower still, I sucked in a breath, realizing what he was about to do.

Flashing my eyes open, I gazed between my legs, watching his icy digit slowly slip inside me. My head rolled back and I dug my nails into Jack's shoulders, panting at the icy hot bliss surging through my core.

Jack growled, pumping in and out of me now before lowering his lips to my ear. "You're chilled perfection. Not warm at all."

Blinking, unsure if I could manage a coherent sentence, I peered at him. "Not warm? Is that a bad thing?"

A second icy finger slipped in, filling me more, and I whimpered.

"It's an *amazing* thing, faerie. Heat makes me uncomfortable. I *hate* it." Jack fucked me with his fingers, his bicep bulging with every thrust. "It's always been a need to satisfy my creature, and it's always nearly driven me mad. But not with you, Sylvie." Jack kissed my jaw, my cheek, my nose, before feathering his lips against mine. "Not with my mate."

The euphoria built and built until reaching its peak. I cried out, shuddering through my release. A whimper bubbled at the back of my throat when Jack removed his fingers, the emptiness devastating.

I traced my fingers over his ice beard, fighting the urge to slump to the ground in a satiated heap. "I never knew it could feel that good."

"Sylvaria," Jack whispered, gravelly and rough. "You have *no* idea."

Wrapping my hand around the back of his neck, I pulled him to me, kissing him, devouring him, hungry for more and more and whatever else he could give me. "Show me."

A wicked grin slid over Jack's lips, and he grabbed both of my calves from the water, propping them on the moss. He took one of my legs and stretched it to one side, pulling the other in the opposite direction so it dangled in the pool. Jack cupped one of my ass cheeks, kneading it, before lifting it to reveal my pussy to him. A guttural groan escaped his chest as he ogled me. I leaned back on my elbows, furiously biting my bottom lip.

Jack positioned himself at my entrance, and I stared at the glowing cerulean veins pulsing faster, matching his racing heart. He slowly pushed inside me, locking his gaze with mine, watching my every reaction, my body language. I winced when the head went all the way in, partially from the momentary discomfort, but mostly because I didn't want it to happen to him. Not Jack. Not my mate.

Jack paused and tilted his head, waiting until my expression relaxed before he pushed more of himself in. He massaged my ass, the other hand squeezing my breast and tweaking the nipple. "Relax, Sylvie." He circled a thumb over my cheek, dragging it past my bottom lip, and catching on it. "You can't give frostbite to the winter *king*."

Jack drove the rest of the way into me, and my back arched, wings flapping so fiercely they fanned my hair. He held onto my hip for purchase, thrusting slowly at first, letting me get acclimated not only to having a male entirely inside me for the first time, but to the sheer *girth* of him. The chill from his cock sent jolts of icy bliss through my core. I'd been gripping tightly around him, but when I eased up, allowing the sensations of him rocking in and out of me, rubbing that sensitive spot at the center, Jack picked up the pace. He slammed into me now, his hips slapping against my ass, over and over.

I reached for his corded forearm, digging my fingers into it, my breath turning into gasping pants. When the now more familiar sensation built this time, it shot so far as my toes, making them curl. I was so close—right there, and Jack, with a devilish smile, *stopped*.

"What are you doing?" I breathed out, my chest heaving, and I fought the urge to *strangle* him.

"Not yet, my little arctic fox," he crooned, spreading me wide and settling between my thighs.

Lying back to enjoy the view, I scraped my nails down his stomach. "You're not the boss of me."

"Don't act as if you don't *like* it," Jack snarled, pushing into me to the hilt again. He hitched one knee by his side and rolled his hips—and winter's blessing, the *friction*, the ever-tightening tension building in my core, had me groaning. "In fact, I think you've liked my commandeering attitude from the beginning.

Haven't you?"

Jack asked a question, I heard him, but this felt too fucking good to miss even one delicious moment of it. Moaning, digging my nails into his chest, I replied with a breathy, "Yes."

"And my creature," Jack continued, lowering his head to suck on my neck. "You like him too, don't you?"

Fucking goddesses, I did. His creature was all-powerful, monstrous, protective, and all *mine*.

"Yes, Jakzair," I moaned, moving my hands to his muscular, plump ass and squeezing it. "Yes."

Jack let out a relieved sigh into my hair. "You're perfect, Sylvie. Fucking. Perfect."

Tears filled my eyes at that. Having lived so many years being told I was anything but perfect and more of a liability and a threat, Jack didn't know how much those words meant to me.

"Use your magic." Jack grazed his canines over my nape, and I stilled, wondering if he was going to bite me there. Was I ready to be claimed? To fully see this through that fast? "You can't hurt anyone or anything in these woods. *Use* it."

The last words weren't a question, they were a fucking command. One, I was more than willing to follow. I'd never let loose with my powers, never explored what they could do for fear of destroying everything.

When Jack flicked his thumb against my clit in tandem with his ferocious thrusts, I came completely undone. Screaming through my release, my magic responded with me, ice spires plunging from the earth around us and rising so high they pierced through the tree branches. Jack pumped three more times, his cock suddenly thickening inside me, *sealing* us together. I never thought I could feel this *full*. When Jack spilled himself, his back arched, head tilting back to let out his creature's roar.

The sight of it made my magic flutter over my skin, patterning glowing ice chips down the length of my body. Additional patches formed on my cheeks, neck, and forehead, chilling my skin and soothing me.

When he came down from his high, Jack peered at me with those ethereal, icy eyes. His brow bobbed at my magic had done— the deadly spires, the new skin. Jack gripped my chin with one hand and bent to kiss me, pooling his own wintry magic into me and adding to my icy patterns, blue snowflakes, and silver dust.

"I *curse* myself for ever questioning you as my mate, Sylvaria." Jack searched my face as if he feared I'd despise him for that.

Pinching my knees against his ribs, I pulled him closer, the water from the hot spring sloshing and steaming. "You have a long time to make it up to me."

Jack nodded, his hand gliding down my neck until it rested on the crook, his finger lazily tracing over my skin, mesmerized by it. "And I see no reason why we should wait on me *claiming* you."

Sudden panic tore the euphoria from me like a snapping twig. "Wait, what?"

Jack arched a brow and frowned before slowly pulling out of me. He said nothing and grimaced at the heat wafting from the pool.

Slipping into the hot spring and resting a hand on his shoulder, I gulped. "Jack, we just got together. We just got over this hurdle of accepting we're mates. Why do you want to rush this?"

Jack still kept silent, his hands wringing together, icy barbs forming over his knuckles.

"What aren't you telling me? And I want the *truth*, Jakzair."

Twenty-Two

Jack

There were two sides to me: the confident, righteous King Jakzair, and then there was Jack, the village idiot. Why hadn't I picked a better moment to say something to her? Directly after we fucked for the first time, *wasn't* it. I didn't want to tell her like this, but honestly, how else should I have seen this playing out? If I had rushed into saying I had limited time in this realm, she'd have questioned my motives. Then again, keeping it from her was bound to have consequences. *Fuck.*

After inhaling a deep, calming breath, I rubbed my knuckles, willing the ice to melt from them. Sylvie kept a hand on my arm so that we could stay in the hot spring, naked and satiated. Lifting my eyes to hers, I raised my chin and bit the bullet. "Every winter solstice, I'm granted time away from my kingdom to search for my mate. The portal that opens is always to somewhere fatedly chosen at random."

"This time—it brought you to the Cove? You hadn't been here before that?" Sylvie's wings fanned slowly, mimicking her gradual understanding.

"That's right." Inching closer, I cupped her face with both hands, urging her to keep looking at me, to understand. "But I can't stay away from my kingdom for long. There's always a *time* limit."

The skin between Sylvie's eyes wrinkled, her bottom lip quivering as if she tried to find the right words to respond to this. "What are you trying to say?"

"I only have two more days, Sylvie." It was like an ice spike driving through my insides from the heart down. Rushing her had never been my intention, and I loathed myself for the perplexed, hurt look on her face now.

Sylvie turned away, her hand dropping from my shoulder. "Two *days?*"

I wanted to tighten my grip on her face, to keep her in place so we could talk this through, but knew she needed to process it.

"Yes. I need to be with my mate *fully* before I return and am allowed no additional time." The icy barbs edged over my knuckles, knowing this clause hadn't always been the case. Deidre was to blame for that.

It didn't take long for the heat to start boiling my insides, but I ignored it the best I could, letting the sweat beads pool on my skin. Where Sylvie was, I was, and that meant staying in the hot spring no matter how unbearable it became.

"And if you don't? Do you get the next solstice to find another mate?" Sylvie kept her back to me, her arms wrapping around herself and covering her breasts.

Sweat dripped from my upper lip, melting the beast's icy beard from my chin. "I have no other mate, Sylvaria. If I return without our bond in place, then every winter becomes simply a break from my duties as king."

"There has to be more to it," she said, almost haughtily. Sylvie turned, sending erratic ripples in the milky waters. "Tell me everything. Because what I'm hearing is that you held this from me until the last minute so that I'd feel guilty if I didn't agree to it."

Questioning my motives. Even suspecting it couldn't prepare me for the harsh reality.

A sharp pain stung at the base of my neck. "That wasn't my intention. I didn't tell you in the beginning because I didn't want you to pity me. To potentially choose it only because of the timeline." My vision sporadically blurred, the sweat pooling through my hair now, melting the ice there too.

"You should have given me the choice, Jack." Sylvie's lips tightened, her wings and ears drooping. Sloshing through the water, she lifted a shaking hand and rested it lightly on my arm, allowing me instant, cool relief.

Letting out a rolling sigh, I resisted hugging her against me to bask in more of her winter's chill. "If I don't return with the bond settled, then I'm destined to live the rest of my life alone. But I'd happily do it, Sylvie, if this *isn't* something you want."

Tears welled in Sylvie's eyes, and she slammed her forehead against my chest. She sniffled several times, lightly punched my stomach, and let her shoulders slump. "Damn you. I like you, Jack. I do want you. Everything in me screams for you."

Gently stroking her hair, I held her because I really wasn't sure what else to do. "Then what's holding you back?"

"So little and yet so much," she whispered, scooting closer until our bodies pressed against each other.

"I have two days. Take tomorrow and think about it. But please don't let my outcome sway you into a future you can't see yourself in. I've spent centuries alone. What's a few more, hm?" I'd meant every word of it, but the thought of enduring even the time until the next solstice without her by my side had nausea curdling my stomach.

"I appreciate you thinking of me like that, and I'm going to take you up on it if only to clear my head. Not surprisingly—" Sylvie leaned back, a weakened smile poised on her lips. "—but you're a hell of a distraction." Her eyes roamed my face. "What happened to the ice?"

"If you think I'm not a fan of the heat, my creature is far worse." Pinching her chin between thumb and forefinger, I pressed a light kiss to her mouth.

Sylvie licked my taste from her lips, her gaze still hooded from our escapades. "Before I painstakingly take my leave of you to think on all of this, I have one question."

"What is it?"

"Those creatures that attacked us—"

And here I hoped she'd forgotten all about them.

"Frost goblins," I offered.

"Sure, yes, the frost goblins. Is that sort of thing normal for you? Should I expect to be fending them off once a week? Every fortnight?"

Despite the disturbing possibility that Sylvie could say no to our bond, I still managed to chuckle. I never found anything adorable, but the way Sylvie squinted one eye and the little tilts of her eyebrows made when she became nervous were the most adorable things I'd ever seen.

"They're not normal, no. The only place they reside is on the outskirts of my kingdom, where all citizens are prohibited from going due to its dangers. They've never made it past the walls, let alone into the castle."

Sylvie nodded, her wings perking up. "And yet they made it *here*?"

Deidre. I still hadn't told her about the fucking Snow Queen, but she'd never even have to meet her, would never have to know she existed, if I simply held onto my crown with Sylvie as my queen.

"I'm not the only magical entity in the realm, but I am the most powerful. The goblins were clearly sent as a distraction."

"From what?" Sylvie's violet eyes widened.

Igniting an icy hot vibrance in my gaze, I replied, "From you."

"There are people who don't want to see you mated, aren't there?" Sylvie rested a hand on my chest, pulsing more chilly magic into my bones.

My mate was so damn intuitive.

"There will always be those, no matter how much power you have, who wish to see you fall just because it makes them feel better. They know I'm powerful and with a mate?" I wrapped a hand around her hip. "Tenfold. As *you* would be."

Sylvie let her bottom lip roll between her teeth. "Arcane Cove has been the first place I've truly felt at home, Jack. I feel settled, and now you're asking me to uproot my life again. I'm happy here."

This was making me far more nervous than I could have predicted. I have always been confident, steadfast, and sure of my actions. The actual fear that someone might not choose me, that my fate lay solely in their hands, knocked my world off its axis.

Norway. She'd mentioned living in Norway all her life before here. My kingdom appeared as if plucked from modern Scandinavia.

"Understandable, but you must miss something about Norway. It's a beautiful country."

Sylvie's amethyst eyes lit up. "It is. I do miss the mountains, the half-frozen waterfalls in the winter, and don't get me started on the northern lights."

There went that hope springing in my stomach again.

"My kingdom has all of those things, and it's perpetually winter. Constant half-frozen waterfalls and the colors of the aurora borealis never abandon the skies." Tracing my thumbs down her neck, I searched her unreadable expression, and it damn near drove me mad.

"That sounds amazing," she whispered, her hands squeezing my biceps.

"You were meant for more in this celestial life, faerie. You said it yourself, your own people cast you out because you were different from them. Did you ever stop to think *why* that was?"

For every moment I thought I gained more of her favor, there were another three moments I could see her drifting away. A constant battle raged in her mind, and I was running out of ammunition.

"I have, but then the Cove found me. The bakery found me. And these people, Jack?" Sylvie lifted her gaze to mine, her grip tightening on my arms. "They have done everything but cast me out. They've welcomed me with open arms."

From her words and the strain in her voice, it was almost as if she was trying to decipher if, when the time came, she'd be able to say goodbye to them. Was that what this was all about?

"Sylv, from the way you're talking, it's as if you'd never see this place or your friends again." I brushed my fingertips across her cheek.

Sylvie blinked, the skin beneath her eyes crinkling. "I figured I'd have to move to your kingdom. Wouldn't I?"

Winter's fucking blessing, that *was* what this was all about. If this had been all it took, I would've reassured her of this days ago.

Chuckling, I gave her lips a quick peck. "Yes, you'd be queen and my mate, but you'd always have access to come back here. Fuck, I wouldn't care if you wanted to pull double duty and still work at the bakery from time to time."

My heart sank when her reaction wasn't as elated as I'd expected.

"I really thought—" She started, but trailed off. Intrigue played majestically in her eyes for a brief moment before sadness and uncertainty won, her gaze falling. "Give me until sundown tomorrow. Is that alright?"

The creature stirred at the mention of a delay, punching at my skull.

"Of course. I'd say to take as much time as you needed, but—"

Sylvie pressed a hand to my cheek. "I know, Frosty."

I swear they could have written hymns about her smile.

We'd crawled from the pool, conjuring clothes for ourselves and sharing last-minute, fleeting kisses before she rode away on Fintan. Nanok emerged from the thick of the forest. I didn't hesitate to lean on him, putting all of my weight on him because I was tired of carrying it all myself. Sylvie was free to choose as she pleased, and I'd respect it, but I'd be lying through my frozen heart if I said I didn't yearn for her to choose *us*.

Twenty-Three

Sylvie

The swirling patterns of a tray of cinnamon rolls had me in a trance. The longer I stared at them, the more it pulled me in despite the conversation and high-pitched shrills of delight from the half a dozen women parading through my bakery. Chelsea's coven sister, Brigid, was having a bachelorette party of sorts to celebrate her official upcoming mating ceremony to a male demon named Lyzur.

"What's that smell?" One of the women asked, snapping me from my thoughts.

Black smoke puffed from the kitchen, and I shrieked, "Oh, no, not the apple fritters." Sprinting to the back, I coughed from the smoke hitting me in the face and waved my arms. Chelsea had followed behind me, gagging, no sooner had she walked through the door.

Sobbing, I whipped open the oven and grabbed the tray with a nearby towel, then tossed it onto the stove top. I started flicking the switches for the overhead vents, but the smoke had already begun to clear.

Brigid stood at the entrance with her hands outstretched, syphoning the smoke from the room with a sympathetic smile.

Sighing, holding back tears, I threw the towel onto the counter and leaned on it. "I'm sorry, ladies, they're burnt to a crisp."

Heels clicked on the floor behind me, and a hand rested on my shoulder. "Sylv, you okay? It isn't like you to let something burn."

This was the *second* time I'd burned something in the past few days.

There was a room full of females from all walks of life and species, some younger than me, some older. It was a golden opportunity to gain perspective on this entire snowy shitstorm.

"Can I run something by you all?" I whipped around to face them.

"Oo, girl talk. That wasn't on the agenda. I'm intrigued," Brigid's sister, Amara, said, helping herself to abandoned cookie dough in a bowl, scooping some with her finger.

Brigid moved beside Chelsea, her plastic tiara glittering with fake gemstones and a thin pink veil. "We're all ears."

Stretching my wings wide like one would their arms, I settled them behind me before beginning. "I found my mate, but it's incredibly complicated."

"When isn't it?" Amara snorted.

"When we first met, he couldn't believe I was his mate. Mostly because I work in a bakery."

Chelsea raised her hand like a child in school.

"You don't have to do that. Chime in whenever you want, Chels."

"I already don't like him if he has a thing against confectionery treats," Chelsea said, looking around the group for affirmation.

"No, no. He loves my treats—"

Amara snorted again, frowning when everyone turned to look at her with a glob of cookie dough halfway to her mouth.

"—he's a winter king. The heat makes him highly

uncomfortable. To him, there was no possible way that I could be his mate because of that, and the fact that he thought I was ashamed of being fae because I hid my ears. His wariness toward me made me wary of *him*."

"And you *didn't* dislike him at first? Do you still dislike him?" Chelsea asked, adjusting the tilted tiara on Brigid's head.

"No, I don't. But he hid the fact that I have to make the claiming choice by *tomorrow*." I wanted to feel the anger, heat flushing my cheeks, and it made me all the more agitated.

"That is pretty shitty," one of the other females said.

"Exactly. It puts so much pressure on me."

The part that jarred me the most was the idea that, if Jack had told me the truth earlier, things would be different. But I couldn't be certain that I wouldn't have thought he had some agenda then or now.

"Does it, though?" Brigid asked, cocking her head to the side and making her tiara topple again. Chelsea was quick to fix it. "Do you not want him?"

Our time in the hot springs had an ache surging through my core, my body betraying me, urging me to say yes, so we could do that repeatedly.

"I *do* want him. I just—" Pausing, I pinched the bridge of my nose and fanned my wings to kick air around. "—I didn't want to feel rushed into it."

Brigid, the oldest of us all and clearly happy to take on the motherly role, moved forward. She clasped her hands with mine and smiled warmly. "What is it they say about love? That it's one of the greatest leaps of faith? Sometimes we don't get to make the hard choices in a timeframe that's convenient for us."

I hardly knew the witch in front of me, but somehow experienced a connection with her like we'd met centuries ago. My sinuses stung and I sniffled. "May I hug you?"

The females around me all laughed, including Brigid, who opened her arms wide. "What kind of question is that? We're all sisters here. Witch or not."

We hugged, and I tried desperately not to blubber on her shoulder. When we peeled away, I eyed her tiara, and in a meek voice, asked, "Would you mind if I tried that on?"

"That's right. Homegirl here bagged herself a king," Amara said, frowning when she noticed the bowl of cookie dough was empty.

Brigid, still smiling, removed the crown and nestled it on my head, pointing at my dingy mirror hanging in the corner. "Go take a look."

It'd been so long since I stared at my reflection. Seeing myself proudly displaying the points of my ears, my wings flared, made me choke on my own breath. I hadn't seen myself that confident in such a long time, I'd forgotten what it looked like on me. I moved my gaze to the tiara, envisioning how a winter queen's crown might appear—how I'd complement the throne *and* Jack's side.

Chelsea's head appeared on my shoulder, her hands gripping my biceps. "What a queen you'll be, Sylvie."

The words hit me with a burst of sizzling electricity aimed at the base of my spine, surging up until they struck my mind. Jack had said those exact words to me.

I turned to look at her, confused as to whether her magic was somehow able to pull that from my memories, but her expression said the contrary.

Chelsea leaned back and eyed me like a tuskless orc. "Sylvie? Why are you looking at me like that?"

154

"Jack said that to me once." An overwhelming sense of relief, gratitude, and excitement hit me like an avalanche. "I've got to go." Laughing, I tore off the tiara to hand back to Brigid and quickly untied my apron, tossing it wherever it landed. "There are a dozen pink and white cupcakes in the display case. You're welcome to them because of the fritters. But be warned, they're laced with extra happy dust, if you get my drift."

"Point me at them," Amara said, making grabby-hand gestures.

Chelsea rested her hands on her hips, watching me shimmy around the kitchen like someone who couldn't keep their head straight. "I take it you made up your mind?"

"Yes," I yelled, smiling so wide it made my cheeks hurt. "Will you give this to Aegean. He should be showing up for his night shift within the hour. I'm sorry. I just really need to go."

"We understand. Go, go. Time is literally of the essence," Chelsea encouraged, whisking her hands toward the door.

"Congratulations, Brigid," was the last thing I said, giving her a quick peck on the cheek, before sprinting outside.

The snow fell in droves so thick they created a whiteout, and I could scarcely see where the tree line started. The wind blew so fiercely it caught my wings, pulling me backward, despite digging my heels into the ground. I'd never seen this depth of a storm in the Cove in the years I'd been here. Was it Jack's doing? Was he upset?

The idea of Jack's emotions causing a blizzard, hurt, and hope over if I'd return to him, if I'd accept him, had me pushing against it. My wings were only slowing me down, so I hid them, using my hand to shield my eyes from the snowflakes flying into them. Faint lights glowed through the falling snow from gas lamps lit in the plaza. I prayed no townspeople were caught in the storm because, despite the wind fighting against me, the cold *I* could handle.

"Fintan," I shouted, squinting against the blinding, snowy wall surrounding me.

I left the bakery behind me, and now that too had disappeared from view. I was at winter's mercy now, not knowing which direction I should head. Did being mates give us some form of connection? Would I be able to feel him? Smell him? Would I be able to let any of it guide me?

Nervously rubbing the tip of my ear, I turned in circles, slight panic rising. "Fintan," I yelled again, my voice cracking.

When only the sounds of the whistling wind answered, I cupped my hands over my mouth and screamed, "Jack."

It was so deadly quiet I could hear my own frantic gasps. A knot formed in my throat as I stifled sobs.

"Nanok," I whispered, not bothering to yell it this time because I knew the wind would only swallow it, sacrificing it to the curtains of snow.

All I wanted to hear were hooves, paws, or feet crunching quickly through the snow. Winter could be as cruel as she was beautiful, blessing me with anything but what I wanted. Did it seek revenge for how long I'd ignored the magic it bestowed on me?

We were so close. I finally realized Jack's words were out of relief and awe. He'd been searching for me for so long and had no trouble envisioning me as his queen, his mate, his forever.

I collapsed to my knees, sucking in a sobbing breath as I landed in a mound of snow up to my shoulders. The ground shook beneath me, and tears seized from the tremors vibrating my bones. I started to crawl away, but the snow gave way beneath me and I fell into an onyx abyss.

Twenty-Four

Jack

"Nanok," I yelled, swirling my magic around myself to keep a barrier between me and this winter's forsaken blizzard. "Stay close to me. You blend in too much."

The snow had inexplicably come out of nowhere only moments ago, and it had nothing to do with me. Though the complexity and magnitude of it had me wishing it were. Nanok sprinted to my side, clinging to my hip, and I trickled my magic around him, shielding us in the same barrier.

My heart stopped. What if Sylvie had been caught in this? She should've still been in the bakery, but what if something called her away? I furiously rubbed my beard and paced in a circle, Nanok following at my side. I promised I'd give her until sunup tomorrow, and that's precisely what I intended to do. The only comfort I had was that she could withstand the cold.

Hooves pounding against the ground echoed off surrounding trees, and I whirled to find Fintan scrambling toward us, his large brown eyes wide with fear. His black nose twitched, sniffing the air and scenting us, but he couldn't *see* us.

"Whoa, boy, whoa," I shouted. "Follow my voice."

Fintan's ears flipped forward, and he ducked his head low, edging toward us. Once his head bumped into my shoulder, he let out an excited huff, his antlers shimmying. I gave calming strokes over his head and neck, securing the barrier around him as well.

"You're fine, Fintan," I soothed.

With both animals huddling under my arms, we braved the winds, and all I could do was wait. Not only for the storm I had no control over, but for the sun to set. Sylvie would either come running to my arms or I'd be met with nothing. It was an unsettling possibility I'd have to come to grips with. She built a life in Arcane Cove and found a place that made her happy and accepted her after being cast out by her own people. It was a lot to ask for her to whisk off to live as a queen in a winter wonderland castle. Though the selfish part of me couldn't fully understand that last part because I'd always had the amenities, the life.

At least the universe had a sense of humor. It took me decades of ethereal life with the promise since my creation that I'd meet my mate. When year after year passed and decades turned into centuries spanning over a thousand years, I molded this icy shield around my heart. Whether it was to protect it or more to protect *me* from the overwhelming disappointment that it could never happen, I still wasn't certain.

I thought my heart would still be guarded when I met Sylvie. That I'd be brazen and cold, if need be, to protect my kingdom at any cost. But the funny part was, when she touched me for the first time, parts of that shield melted, inviting her right the fuck in.

It started as a smirk, transmuted into a chuckle, and, before long, erupted into uncontrollable, maniacal laughter. Nanok and Fintan turned their heads toward me simultaneously, eyeing the barrier I kept up for them, probably wondering if braving the storm was safer than being trapped in a small space with a madman. I laughed so hard that tears pushed from the corners of my eyes, freezing once they reached my skin.

Sucking in a breath, I calmed the chuckling and sighed, rubbing my knuckles at my eyes. A few laughs still fluttered from my chest, but eventually I stopped them altogether. "Sorry, boys, I was just having a little go at the irony of all of this."

Nanok stared at me unenthused, smacking his lips together. If he were a humanoid, I could envision his large eyes rolling profusely into his skull.

"Oh, shut up, you overgrown, furry—" I started, but froze when I felt it—the discomforting pang at the back of my head, similar to the day I met Sylvie. "No," I breathed out, fanning my palm at the barrier to move with me as I stormed further into the woods.

"Sylvie?" I shouted into the snow.

Fintan went on alert, sniffing the air furiously around us and whimpering. I joined him, smelling for that distinguishable scent and detecting it a moment too late. No sooner had I sensed her presence than it was yanked from my gut by an enchanted, invisible rope—something *took* her.

"Winter's curse, no," I roared, grabbing my head and pacing around the two animals.

If it wasn't enough that someone took Sylvie, it was the gut-wrenching realization that I knew precisely where she was and the risk it meant to go after her. She was in my realm. It created a very, very short list of possible places she could be. What was worse, given the time constraint, I couldn't be certain where the lake portal would take me, or if I'd be able to get back.

Frowning, I turned to Nanok, who was sitting with his hind feet sticking out. His held his head low, and his ears drooped, already knowing what was about to happen. "Nanok, friend, I don't want to risk you not having a home. I have to go after her. Can you understand that?"

Lifting his chin, Nanok closed and opened his eyes with a huff.

"Thank you, boy," I squeezed out, ruffling Nanok's head and ears. "I'll take you both to the frost giant's cave. You keep each other safe until the storm clears. That goes for you, too, Fintan." Pointing at the stag, I waited for him to bow his head.

With my and my mate's animal companions in tow, I led them to the icy cave, finding comfort in having a sanctuary in the blizzard. They were both magical winter beings, but I didn't care to test their resolve against *other* creatures taking advantage of the blinding snow. After kissing Nanok's head, praying it wasn't the last time I'd see him, I made for the lake.

Anger fueled my steps, squinting against the flakes collecting on my lashes and ignoring the snow making my shirt damp. Once I reached the bank, I pressed my fingertips to my chest, making the clothes disappear, and slid my feet into the water.

"Leaving already?" A familiar voice croaked.

The same shorter being with the long, bushy, black beard from when I'd arrived sat on a stool on the ice, fishing. Only this time, they sat underneath the shelter of a small tent, with something steaming and wrapped in a blanket resting on their lap. Unlike before, they appeared unperturbed by my nudity.

"I'll be back," I proclaimed. "There's something I need to take care of first."

Diving into the water, the freezing chill coating my skin and relieving my aching bones, I let the cold power my movements. My mate was in trouble before we'd had the chance to claim one another, to bond to each other fully. There was only *one* person who wished to see us fail, and *she* was about to feel the true wrath of Jack Frost, the wrath of King Jakzair.

Sylvaria was *my queen*.

Twenty-Five

Sylvie

The first few seconds were like falling through an endless black hole before I landed in a pile of something fluffy and white. Sputtering from it, collecting on my lips and scattering my hair, I scooped some into my palm. It looked like hundreds of tiny Styrofoam pieces. When I tipped my palm to discard them, they floated away rather than falling, and some stuck to my skin. Squinting skyward, I expected to see clouds mixed into gray or blue, but an ample distorted light was there instead.

"What in the—" I started, slumping forward and halting at the sight of a snowman—the perfect kind, with three proportionate snow balls, a carrot for a nose, coal for eyes, and buttons, red hat, red scarf, the whole deal. Next to it was a cozy cottage, but it wasn't mine.

Swallowing a coarse lump forming in my throat, I reached for the house and gasped, recoiling my hand. It wasn't wood or stone, it was smooth like *plastic*. With a shaky arm, I stretched my fingers toward the snowman next, expecting it to be wet and cold. Tears blurred my vision when the generic material pressed to my skin. It, too, was plastic.

"Oh, good, you're finally here," a woman's voice boomed, thick with a British accent.

I covered my ears from how loud she sounded. It was almost as if she were standing on a ladder, using a megaphone pointed down at me. Turning circles, kicking the fake confetti snow around me, I fell back on my ass when a giant face appeared, distorted like the sky.

The woman cackled at the sight of me falling, and a humongous finger tapped the distortion, shaking the ground beneath me. I grabbed the ground for purchase, terror wrenching my spine.

"Isn't it ingenious?" The woman asked, her face disappearing, but both hands appeared on each side of me now, and she *lifted* me.

No. I wasn't. Am I in a fucking snow globe?

"I thought it fitting considering what we all are," the woman added, laughing as she turned the globe upside down.

The snowman and house stood still, but the snow I sat in fell to the bottom, taking me with it. I furiously flapped my wings, floating in the middle of the globe in case she turned it again.

"Damn. I forgot you had those." She turned the globe again, and once she rested it on a hard surface, I eased myself back to the fake snow. "But look at you. Your wings are out, even your ears. Good for *you*, darling."

"Who are you?" I yelled, clenching my fists at my sides.

The woman leaned back and flicked the globe, making it shake, but I widened my stance to keep from falling this time.

"No need to shout, my word. Are you trying to give me a headache?" The woman rubbed her temple. It was hard to make out her features from the distortion of the glass, but her eyes were blood red, her hair long and grey, and something black streaked her cheeks.

Saying nothing, I sprinted to one side and outstretched my arm when the glass got closer. I pressed my palms to it, feeling up and down. It really was a glass globe without the usually added water solution—an exclusion I was presently grateful for.

"I'm surprised dear old Jack hasn't mentioned me by now." The woman propped her elbow on whatever surface the globe was on, resting her chin in her palm.

My core fluttered at the mention of him—my mate. I pressed a hand to my chest and whirled to face her. "You know Jack?"

"Of course, I do. Where in blazes do you think you are?" The woman flicked her fingernails around the globe, and I could scarcely make out their pointy length. "You're in the winter kingdom, my dear. And *I'm* its Snow Queen."

A million thoughts raced through my mind at once, so obtrusive that I had to grip my skull to get it all to slow down. Queen? I thought Jack said there wasn't a queen. Did she want Jack for herself?

Growling in frustration, I sprinted to the other side, beating my fists against the glass once I'd reached it. "I don't understand. Jack said there is no queen."

The woman scoffed. "Yes, yes. Jack is the Winter King, in the head palace of this realm. But—" She moved her face closer and I backed away, alarmed at the sight of black ooze running down her cheeks and dripping from her chin. "—not for long."

She didn't want Jack. She wanted what he *had*.

A deep sigh pushed from my lungs. Jack hadn't told me everything. I wanted to be angry at him for it, but all I could process at the moment was the sinking realization that I might never see him again, *to* be furious with him.

"Who are you?" I asked again, desiring to know more than simply the Snow Queen.

The woman removed something from her head and rested it near the globe. It had black, spiked designs, and the material glistened from the light source hung overhead. "My name is Diedre. And I'm the rightful heir to the Winter throne, not *Jakzair*."

She'd said his name with such venom it made my skin crawl. With my fingertips pressed to the glass, I walked the perimeter of the globe, frowning when I completed a full circle. There was no means of escape.

"Jack said he was born into it. Created for that sole purpose. How could you possibly be its rightful ruler?" I shuffled my feet through the white confetti, hoping by some twist there was a trap door or something.

Diedre slammed her fist near the globe, making it wobble, and I stumbled forward, steadying myself against the glass. "He was. His sole purpose was to convince the people that he would be a more righteous leader. I swear, you order one too many executions and suddenly everyone sees you no longer fit for the throne." Sighing, she ran her fingers over the crown she'd rested on the table. "The people voted for Jack, and I received this kingdom, on the outskirts of the realm. Smaller. More glum. All but *forgotten*." Diedre smacked the crown with a sneer, launching it away, and making it clang to the floor.

What was I supposed to say in this instance? Executing people. The anger I could feel swelling from her very essence. The people were right about Jack being a more benevolent king. Diedre shouldn't be allowed near it, but I also needed out of here.

"That's a hard go, Diedre. But what do I have to do with any of this?"

Diedre's crimson eyes blazed before her face pressed to the glass, a lethal fingernail pointing at me through it. "You are my undoing as much as you are my salvation, Sylvaria. He's been searching for you for centuries, and I honestly hoped he'd find you so you would *reject* him."

Moving to the opposing side, I pressed my fingertips to the glass, coursing my magic through it. Frost coated it, the chill settling in, but it wouldn't crack as I'd hoped. I kept silent. The thought of Jack's expression when he suspected I wouldn't go through with this tore at my gut, let alone the idea of how he'd look if I wholly rejected him to his *face*.

"It was all going according to plan, but no, the little winter faerie had to go and develop feelings for the king. Swoon over him." Diedre gagged and pinched the bridge of her nose. "My word, you even fucked him."

Feelings. Had I?

"I put a curse on Jakzair, you see," Diedre continued, yanking me from my thoughts, entirely focused on her again. "Before it, he had more time to search for his mate every year, but I'm impatient, so I halved it. Because *if* he found her, surely it wouldn't be enough to convince her to be claimed."

With each passing word from Diedre, with each breath of confession, the coal building in my throat grew larger. My limbs were numbing, and I slid down the glass until I met with the confetti snow.

"And when his mate rejected him and the time lapsed—"

"You become the Winter Queen," I whispered, finishing for her.

Diedre snapped her twig-like fingers. "You're smarter than you look. And so, you see, you are to remain here until time is up to ensure that doesn't happen. After that, I'll gladly whisk you back to your pitiful excuse for a little ramshackle town."

It couldn't end like this, could it? All because of one being's desire for more power? Power she *shouldn't* have? Couldn't have?

I leapt to my feet, flapping my wings to bring me closer to her face, glaring at her through the glass. "You won't be queen, Diedre."

"As much as I appreciate your confidence, faerie. Time says otherwise." Diedre cackled and patted the globe before walking away.

No, no. This couldn't be happening. I never meant for this to happen. If only I hadn't been so stubborn and agreed beforehand, I wouldn't even be here. It would've already been done—but could I really have blamed myself? It all happened *so* fast.

Tears prickled my eyes, and I held my face in my hands.

A loud bang followed by the sound of splintering wood startled me to my feet.

"Diedre," Jack's voice roared, dragging out her name as if commanding her. "Where is she?"

Gasping and in a fit of panic, I beat my hands against the glass. "Jack, I'm here," I shouted at the top of my lungs.

"Whatever do you mean, darling?" Diedre asked, standing in front of the globe and blocking it from view.

"Don't fucking toy with me, witch. *Where is* she?" Jack loomed over her, and despite the haze of the glass, I could see his ice creature forming over his face.

"Jack," I yelled again, kicking the glass over and over. From my vantage point, the sounds echoed off the glass so loudly that it made my ears ring. How could he not hear me?

"Back in her cottage contemplating her life choices, I'd imagine. Whyever did you think she'd be here of all places?" Diedre countered.

Jack growled and stalked around the room, shoving tables aside, pulling books from their shelves.

"You're making a mess and I do not appreciate it," Diedre spat, moving toward him to straighten things in his wake.

The globe was in clear view now, and I beat against it harder, screamed louder, flew in the middle of it, and did this over and over until I was so hoarse I couldn't yell anymore. He never saw it. He never saw me. He had no idea I was *here*.

Twenty-Six

Jack

Diedre could sling her venomous words at me until she was red in the face, but it wouldn't stop me from looking for her. For my mate. My winter faerie. She *was* here—that sweet scent of Sylvie's hung heavy in the air.

"Where *is* she, witch?" Grabbing onto a bookshelf, I glared at Diedre, willing her to test my resolve.

Diedre scratched her long, pointy nails down the length of her neck, trying her best not to look bothered by what I was doing—what I *planned* to do. "Winter's curse, Jakzair. Are you expecting to find her sandwiched between the wall and a bloody bookshelf?"

As much as I despised Diedre's very existence, I couldn't deny how powerful a sorceress she had become. It made Sylvie's disappearance all the more concerning.

"Knowing how you operate, I wouldn't overlook a fleck of *dust*," I roared before toppling over the shelving. Books flew in all directions, cracking spines and bending pages.

A twitch formed in Diedre's cheek, and the hand at her neck balled into a trembling fist. "Face it, Winter King. You've already lost." She'd spat the words, coating them with poison, and pointed to an hourglass dispensing white sand.

The creature wasn't having it, forcing its way out, the icy barbs forming over my forearms, shoulders, and head. Storming toward Diedre, I formed an iced dagger and glowered at her. "I've only lost when the last grain *drops*." I slammed her back against the far wall, pinning her there with the sharpened barbs on my arm and the dagger's blade hovering near her neck. "I won't ask again."

Diedre cackled, scraping her skin against one of my barbs and making a thin line of crimson form there. "Your threats are pointless. We can't kill each other, you know that. We would've done that a long, long time ago if we *could*."

"That's fine," I countered, pressing my fingertips to a painting hanging on the wall behind her. "Killing you would be far too much of a courtesy for what I intend to do until you tell me where. She. *Is*." The canvas froze solid, and I slammed my fist through it, the pieces crumbling into shards.

Diedre's eyes flared, her entire body starting to vibrate. "You infantile asshole. That artist is dead. It was one of the only memories I had of life before becoming queen."

Material possessions had always been the easiest way to work under Diedre's skin. Usually, I wouldn't have resorted to such petty means, but time truly was running out.

"Boo fucking hoo." Extending a hand, I shot icicles through several vases on a table in the corner. "I never *had* a life before being king. So, I sure as freezing hells won't let you rob me of the only chance I have at some semblance of normalcy."

A subtle squeak sounded from Diedre's throat as she watched the priceless vases crack, shatter, and explode from the table. Her gaze lingered in that direction for a breath too long, however, before returning her attention to me. "Are you enjoying this?"

"It requires my still being in your company." A wobbling glass orb on the same table as the vases caught my attention because I could have sworn I saw something flash inside it. "Otherwise, I'd be enjoying it far more."

Diedre made another lightning-fast glance in that same direction and pushed her neck against my icy barb, this time, it fully pierced her skin. "Maybe you're not trying *hard* enough."

Narrowing my eyes at her blood rolling down her neck and collecting on my icy blue hand, I snarled and pushed from the wall. I stormed for the table, shaking remnants of Diedre's blood from my fingers—icy patches formed in the floor, latching onto my feet and momentarily freezing me in place.

Snapping Diedre a glare over my shoulder, her hand poised with tendrils of white and black magic, I yanked my feet free with ease. "You really want to play this game, witch? You know my power transcends yours." I ignored her, turning my attention back to the mysterious globe, and my heart froze over again when I caught that hint of blue wing.

"Oh, really? Who cursed *who* here?" A black vine snapped around my waist, pulling taut and yanking me several meters backward.

Diedre had been gifted with winter magic, the same as the rest of us who were chosen, but the dark magic seduced her, forever condemning her to black ice. I still often wondered if the extra perks to her magic were worth it to Diedre in the end.

"Besides—" Diedre continued, wrapping her pale hand around the vine and reeling me in like a seal. "—all I need to do is *distract* you long enough."

The daunting realization had my monster plunging through my skin, my height now challenging the ceiling, the icy spikes on my shoulders, arms, hips, and head the most pronounced they've been since waging war. I sliced through the vine like a piece of thread and slammed a fist into the floor. My magic surged an icy trail, heading for Diedre until it wrapped up to her neck and held her there.

Turning my back on the snowy witch, it took only three long strides in this form to reach the table. A moderately-sized snow globe rested atop a wooden pedestal. As I crouched to peer inside, there was a snow-covered cottage, a snowman, and a miniature Sylvie flapping her wings erratically and screaming, though I couldn't hear her.

Anger, frustration, fear—it all suffocated me and made my blood sizzle. "You trapped her in a fucking *snow globe*?" I roared, lunging back to Diedre, who'd managed to set her arms free from my wintry trap.

"I personally thought it was quite creative, darling," Diedre mused, clacking her onyx nails together. With her hands released, she fluttered her fingers, melting the ice from her legs in wisps of charcoal and icy dust.

"Get her out of it," I commanded, pointing an icy claw at the orb.

Diedre folded her arms and arched a thin white brow. "No."

Growling, positively fuming, I swept my arms skyward, raising spikes of ice at her sides, spiraling far above her and curling toward her face. "Do it now, witch."

Diedre appeared unfazed as she eyed my wintry handiwork, flicking her nail against one spike. "You've grown quite the temper as of late. Is this what it's like to be mated? All raging hormones without an ounce of sensibility left?"

Through the sight of my creature form, the world took on a glacial blue prism and pristine clarity. The sand in the hourglass left little more than an hour, and soon we'd run out of time without any means to undo it. I reached for the globe.

"If you intend to smash it, I wouldn't advise that, Jakzair," Deidre said, her voice as coy and confident as ever.

Pausing with my hand poised over the orb, Sylvie still yelling at me at the top of her lungs behind the glass, I peered at Diedre. "*Why?*"

"It may look like your typical setting with the quaint cottage and snowy companion." Diedre sauntered toward me, her hands slashing left to right with icy black blades that I effortlessly countered. "But it's actually a trapped crumb from Antarctica. If you smash it, the crumb goes back to where it belongs, and Sylvie goes with it. What was it about that winter king clause again?" She pretended as if she didn't know, tapping her lips.

I had no intention of playing along and stayed silent.

"That's right." Diedre snapped her fingers. "Unless you're mated, you're at the portal's mercy on where it takes you. How long do you think it'd take for you to see Sylvie again when the portal could take you anywhere in the known universe, hm?"

Diedre looked entirely too fucking satisfied with herself. This couldn't have been fate's plan. There *had* to be a loophole to this spell. Keeping my attention on Diedre, I pressed my claws to the globe, coating it with magic and frosting the glass. Sylvie stirred inside, turning circles and raising her hands, already attempting spurts of her own power. It was up to my mate now. Neither of us could get out of this alone, but with our magic combined, we might stand a chance.

Glancing at the dwindling sand in the hourglass, I stifled a sigh, my creature settling until only the spikes at my shoulders, part of my head, and down my forearms remained. "Your ignorance toward mates and foul words against the concept is the precise reason you won't win this, Diedre."

Diedre cackled, bending backward to let her head fall back. After flashing me a steely, crimson glare, she taunted, "Prove it."

Twenty-Seven

Sylvie

Jack had kept looking at the hourglass resting on the table across from mine, but from this angle, I couldn't see how much was left—how much *time* we had left. Jack fought with Diedre, hurling magic and foul words. All I could do was scream, yell, and fly around until he somehow noticed me. If it weren't for Jack smashing those vases and making Diedre nervous, I wasn't sure how long it would've taken him.

Diedre's declaration on the spell cast within the globe confused me. Why would she have stopped Jack from smashing the globe if it would have sent me somewhere Jack couldn't reach me? She'd have won. Plain and simple. Or why hadn't she sent me there in the first place? It was all a game to get into Jack's head because of his devotion to me, his desire to be mine, and to have an eternal soulmate. Diedre failed in her plans because, from this vantage point, I witnessed precisely why I, in turn, wanted to be his *queen*.

Jack's magic frosting the glass made it easier to do something, anything, with my dormant powers. I'd caused an avalanche, surely I could manage breaking the glass of a godsdamned snow globe. Poising my fingers, I recalled the sensations I'd experienced when the icy spires shot through the trees because I *willed* them there. A chilly sort of electric current had started at the base of my spine and surged its way into my skull that day. I'd been elated that I'd found someone like me—another blessed by winter magic. Our touch brought us both *comfort.*

"It should've been mine," Diedre shrieked, launching those same black vines as before, only now they were sharp on the ends like spears.

Jack, in half creature form, deflected them with his shoulder and forearm barbs. With every attack, more of the monster took over, making him taller, wider, and almost entirely composed of ice.

"You let the darkness consume you," Jack roared back. "Did you not think there'd be consequences for your *actions?*"

Concentrating on the way my heart warmed whenever Jack was near me, the blissful chill he brought to my skin and bones, I willed my magic to my fingertips. My wings flapped emphatically as if aiding my power.

The blackness leaking from Diedre's eyes grew more intense, traveling down her neck. She threw spiny vine after vine at Jack over and over, only ever managing to nick some ice chips from his shoulders, which quickly hardened up. "Winter itself bore you because it found me unworthy. If it weren't for *you*, I would be queen of it *all.*"

My arms shook from the effort, and I pinched my eyes shut, attempting to ignore the unfolding scene between this villainess and my mate.

Jack's growls intensified to the point of rattling the globe that entrapped me. "It found you unworthy because you *fucked* up,

Diedre. When will you understand that your fate was of *your* own doing?"

At the same time, Diedre responded with a shriek so shrill it could split mountains, my magic burst from my palms, colliding with the glass and *cracking* it. The sound reverberated in my ears, and I gasped before risking fluttering my eyes open. The pattern fell from top to bottom in zig-zag like an unruly lightning bolt. My wings flicked taut, and I charged forward, wincing as I slammed my shoulder into the globe.

There was a blinding flash of white light and swirl of icy black dust before my knees thumped to the ground, my hands following. I kept my eyes shut from fear of where I'd find myself, but as my fingers grazed splintered wood against my skin, I smiled.

"Sylvaria," Jack cried out.

My wings fanned out, flapping excitedly when I met Jack's glacially glowing blue gaze.

"What in the freezing seven hells?" Diedre cried out, her attention turning on me, black claws raised.

Jack charged toward me in full ice creature form, his arms splayed wide. "Sylvie, hide your wings," he roared.

His words caught me by surprise at first, causing me to hesitate. As I folded them back, willing my wings to disappear, a black vine flew toward me over my shoulder, clipping one wing in the top corner. I wailed, the pain striking into my neck and upper back. Jack wrapped his arms around me, taking more of the voracious vine strikes into his own icy armor. Snow, mist, and ice crystals swirled around us like a wintry tornado. Then suddenly—we disappeared.

Our bodies fell into a slump of chilly, powdery snow. Towering evergreen and silver birch trees hung overhead, their branches weighed heavily with snow. A cardinal perched on one branch, its bright red feathers a stark contrast to the blanket of white. It tilted its head at us, giving a single tweet before a female cardinal flew beside it and the two blissfully took to the skies together.

Sitting up on my elbows, I felt my body as if Jack's snowy magic still entwined me. "How did you do that? Can you appear anywhere you want?"

"No," he responded, his jaw set, and a steely demeanor overtook his features. Jack reached for my wing, healing the torn tip. "I can only go where I can *see* and only in my realm."

A cloud glided overhead, its shape bearing a striking resemblance to that of an hourglass.

Mates.

"Jack," I shouted, scrambling to my knees and already fumbling with my clothes.

Jack stood still, the ice carved into his brow bone furrowing, watching me.

Pausing with my hands at the ties of my blouse, I reached for his mystical creature's face instead. The palm I pressed to his frozen cheek made the ice there shimmer from my touch. "We're running out of time." Pulling the string, I opened the shirt, revealing my breasts to him before slipping it from my shoulders. "You need to claim me, mate. I accept this. I want you. I want all of it."

The glow in Jack's gaze radiated as he roamed my bare breasts. A square patch between his hip bones began to shift. Gulping, because I had no fucking clue what I was in for, I removed the rest of my clothes and flared my wings. The snow was comforting, settling between my toes and embracing my ankles and shins.

Jack moved closer, his height having grown an extra foot from his fae-form. This was the first time I'd seen him like this, when he wasn't fighting, and I'd be lying if I said I wasn't the least bit nervous.

"Sylv, not like—not like this," he whispered with a pained wince, his voice in creature form deeper than the fjord valleys. The icy barbs on his forehead and cheeks sheathed in and out as if Jack and his creature were battling for control.

Tracing my fingers over the overlapping ice flaps appearing like ab muscles at his stomach, I trailed upward until I reached his chest and pressed my palm there, pulsing warmth into him. "Diedre is probably already looking for us. It has to be *now*."

Gulping again, I turned my back to him and slowly bent forward, grabbing my ass cheeks and pulling them apart. My pussy was on full display to him now, and, biting my lip, I spread myself further, inviting him to *take* me. Peeking over my shoulder, a long, thick appendage appeared from the rectangular slit. His cock, too, was pure ice, still retaining the bulbous head, but down the length were several carved ridges. At its base was another rotund portion, double the size of the head. He lurched forward, but paused again, his chest heaving at the sight of me submitting to him.

"Take me, Jack. I'm yours," I whispered, fanning my wings for him and making them sparkle.

Those words struck something feral in him, and he prowled forward, grabbing one of my hips and guiding me to my knees. His other hand moved my head toward the ground, holding me there as the tip of his cock teased my entrance. It was so fucking cold, and I already shivered with anticipation at how it'd feel *inside* me.

As he slowly pushed inside, I let out a raspy gasp, my knees buckling, but Jack's hand on my waist kept me from collapsing into the snow. Just when I thought all of him was in, he pushed the rest of it, that final bulbous end slamming against my ass.

It was so deliciously cold and thick. I never imagined experiencing such a sense of fullness. My insides pulsed and clenched around him, acclimating to the new intrusion, accepting it, wanting more of it. Languidly, he stroked the apex of my wings, rubbing back and forth, making me squeak at the way it made my stomach flutter. He rocked in and out of me, slowly at first, and picking up speed when he felt me relax.

"Oh, fuck," I cried out.

His chilly palm moved from my hip, sliding against my stomach until it reached my breasts, grabbing and kneading one. He thrusted, the icy protrusions at his hips rubbing against my ass, surprising at first but soon *so* welcoming. The ridges on his cock rubbed on and off that sensitive, small area within my core. Every time one brushed, it made me dig my fingers into the snow, grabbing handfuls, pleasurable moans and groans echoing from my throat.

Jack pulled me upward with a palm pressed between my breasts, his lips lowering to my ear. "No other female has taken this cock, Sylvaria." When I tensed at that because how could that be possible, he added, "My *creature's* cock. Do you know why?"

Shuddering, coming fucking undone at the seam for him, I shook my head.

"Because they weren't my mate," he declared, wrapping the words in a claiming snarl. He plowed into me once, hard and rough at the word "mate." "They weren't *you*, faerie. No one else could take my cock but *you*." He brazenly thrust into me again a single time, pausing with our bodies fused, chilly skin to chilly skin. "And especially not *enjoy* it."

Snaking a hand to the back of his neck, I scratched my nails over the ridges of ice that'd replaced his spiky hair. "Fuck me, Frost."

A rumble vibrated in his chest, pulsing through my back, and he fisted my hair, unleashing a long dark blue tongue that I would beg him to use later—after we were mated and safe and eternally together. He licked my cheek and lapped it over my lips, before giving me a frozen kiss and pushing my head back to the ground.

He wrapped a hand around one of my shoulders, the other snatching my wrist and holding my arm captive behind me. His thrusts became positively animalistic, waves of pleasure twisting through me in so many tantalizing knots I couldn't see straight, couldn't think. The climax built like a cracking glacier until it broke away completely, plunging me into frigid waters and sending rapture pulsing through my core. I moaned his name through my release, once for Jack and once for Jakzair.

Jack kept thrusting, his claws pressing to the skin at my breastbone. "I claim you, Sylvaria. You're *mine*." At that, he pushed the bulbous end of his cock inside me, stretching and filling my opening. It hurt for only a moment before the dizzying pleasure had me going boneless.

Arching his back, he spilled inside me—a pleasuring river of chilly essence that had my knees shaking, plunging me into another orgasm. Jack didn't stop there. He kept us connected, his cock pulsing inside me, and an icy hotness sizzled over my skin from where he touched my chest. He leaned over me, his canines grazing my nape before they sank in. It wasn't so much as a bite, however, as it was him lapping and sucking. Glancing down at my chest, a glowing blue tendril formed, creating an intricate pattern around each breast, up and over my collarbones, and didn't stop until it reached just below my chin. Below the dip where my collarbones met, an icy patch matching those of Jack's creature formed in a diamond shape.

Jack's rough nose nuzzled my hair, and he tapped the patch with his claw. "A piece of my true nature will now always be with you, Sylvie." Slowly, he pulled out of me, allowing me to recalibrate myself from the unnerving emptiness it created.

Nibbling my lip, I turned to face him, running my fingers over the glowing patterns on me now, but mostly, the diamond. "This is your mark?"

"Yes." Cracking his neck, he grunted, the monstrous parts of him gradually morphing back into the snowy blonde fae male I'd met in my bakery.

Snapping my wings, I gasped, panic replacing the contented satiation. "Diedre. Jack, we have to—"

Jack pulled me against him, sending snow pluming around us. He wrapped one burly, secure arm around my waist and stroked my hair. "It's alright. We've been rushing through everything because we didn't have a choice. Now?" He kissed the side of my head. "We can slow down. She can't do a fucking thing to us now. Alright?"

I believed him, and a relieved sigh melted from my lungs. Resting my head on his shoulder, I cooed as he gently began to sway us. The forest was quiet, save for the occasional bird chirping, branches rustling, and the subtleness of snowflakes collecting in the trees. We stood naked in these snowy woods, newly mated, and finally had the chance to simply *be*.

Twenty-Eight

Jack

With my creature settled and my heart now thawing, relaxation came to me in a luxurious, chilly wave, making me boneless. I had ported us deep into the woods behind my castle—what was soon to be *our* castle. It could be days before Diedre found us if she bothered to look after the last grain of sand fell. I'd carve that look on her face when she realized she lost, seeing us mated, into my bone marrow. Fuck her. I've been a fair and just king toward her, giving her a kingdom, her own lands. She chose to show her appreciation by cursing me, threatening my crown, *and* my mate. Winter's night only knew the punishment I'd bestow on her, but perhaps still being her ruler with a new queen at my side would be punishment enough.

I sculpted the snow into a lounging bank, our naked forms lying nuzzled against it. Sylvie was curled into the crook of my arm, my fingers making lazy circles on her arm. She rested her head on my chest and played with the snowflake pendant hanging from my neck. Snow fell silently around us, but didn't collect on us from my magical shield. I dared say it was one of the most memorable moments of my celestial existence—for today.

My mark glowed ever brightly on my faerie's chest, its glacial hue matching the colored tips of her hair and making her amethyst eyes radiate. Grinning, one canine poking over my bottom lip, I traced my thumb over the icy diamond patch.

"You look far too satisfied with yourself, Jack," Sylvie mused, her tone calm and sleepy. A smile graced her lips, and she gazed up at me with hooded lids.

"Mm," I groaned, switching to rubbing her chin. "Can you blame me? I've searched for you for so long, Sylvie. To see my mark on my mate. To have you here in my arms, and for you to *accept* me? I'm not sure what else could top it."

Sylvie, still smiling, scraped her nails over my stomach, tracing each curve of my abdominal muscles before trailing to the blonde hair that led to my still hard as packed ice cock. "I can certainly try."

My heart raced as my mate moved to straddle me, her thighs clutching my hips. She positioned my cock at her entrance, the slick, chilly heat of her driving me mad as she slid down, sheathing me inside her. It was a revelation to feel such warmth, not only comforting but godsdamned euphoric. Sylvie rocked her hips back and forth, her insides clenching my length like a fucking vise. I rested my hands on her waist, kneading her there, trying not to let my head fall back the way it wanted. I didn't want to miss one damn glimpse of the beauty writhing on top of me.

Those gorgeous winter wings of hers flapped somberly, their sparkle amplified from the falling snowflakes. Sylvie's lips parted, her hands gripping her hair, and gasps, moans, and whimpers delicately echoed from her throat. When she opened her eyes, a pulsing sky-blue glow replaced the usual violet, my mark radiating so profusely it was almost blinding. I grunted as her thrusts grew more frantic, bringing me ever closer to the edge.

No sooner had Sylvie cried out, exploding through her release, the pulse of it shuddering around my cock, than I tore through my own climax. My back arched from the snow bank, my fingers digging into her hips, my neck and spine tensing. With me still buried inside her, Sylvie leaned forward, her petite fingers tilting my chin upward. Her mouth slightly opened, but instead of kissing me like I thought she would, tendrils of blue, white, and shimmering silver flowed from her lips, traveling into my mouth, down my throat, and settling in my chest.

The inside of my left forearm burned and sizzled before turning icy hot. Sylvie's wings flared excitedly as if they were in on whatever my mate had just done to me. Grinning, Sylvie's eyes turning back to their normal purple hue, she lifted my forearm into view. A winged pattern was carved into my flesh, the bulk of the design on the inside of my arm, wrapping around to the outside. It wasn't created with ink like a tattoo, more like crystals, preserved ice and snow, and bits of Sylvie's magic.

"Now, you too, are mine, Jakzair," Sylvie whispered, petting my new marking with pride.

It was exquisite and uniquely hers.

"You know," I teased, leaning back on the snowbank with my arms propped. "I was already yours; you didn't *have* to take it a step further."

Sylvie danced her fingers up my abs before wrapping her fist around my snowflake charm and holding the chain taut. "A gal can never be too sure." The grin plastered on her face, one of a female who was satisfied, joyous, and enamored with her mate, had my chest going tight.

"Now, who looks far too satisfied with themselves?" Smiling, I curled a hand around her neck and gave her a long, luxurious, universe-consuming kiss. Pulling away, I cinched my brow, hesitant to ask what had been itching my curiosity since she brought it up.

Sylvie sat back on her haunches and tilted her head. "Jack? What is it?" She rubbed the pointed tip of one of my ears, and it was such an effortless, intimate touch that it damn near took my breath away.

"You said your people, the faeries, cast you out because they feared your power. What were they if not winter faeries themselves?" My shoulders tensed after asking, awaiting her answer and fearing she'd either close herself off to me or worse, get angry.

Sylvie sighed and resettled herself so she was lying in my arms again, playing with my abs. She had such a fascination for them, and it was hardly the moment to tease her about it, but eventually I would. "I was the only winter faerie in our community. My parents died when I was a baby. To this day, I'm not entirely sure they were even my birth parents, given what I am, but it started out as my special powers being a gift."

Interlacing our fingers, I pressed a kiss to each of her knuckles. "Do you remember using your magic as a child?"

The skin across her forehead wrinkled, as if she were digging into repressed memories. "Vaguely. But that was such a long time ago. I'd do little tricks like making ice roses or little cars for my friends. We'd chase each other in the forests, and they'd sometimes get mad because my wings were bigger than theirs."

The wings flapped once, and I reached a hand toward them, tracing the edges in an effort to soothe them—to soothe *her*.

"Everyone else's powers were nature-based—flowers, trees, sunlight. I never told anyone that I could create far larger things than small trinkets. In fact, I held back so much that I often wondered if I could make an entire castle if I tried hard enough."

Gently pushing her back by her shoulders so our gazes met, I said, "Why don't you try, then? These woods are the perfect opportunity for you to see what you can do, Syl. Go beyond what you did before."

Her previous fears almost instantaneously had her curling her knees to her chest. "Jack, I don't—"

When she turned her head from me, I brought it back with a single finger under her chin. "Let *go*, Sylvaria. You can't hurt anyone or anything here. What do you have to lose?'"

Determination straightened her face, and she pushed to her feet, hands clenched at her sides and wings pressing together at her back. She turned her gaze to me, brows arching as if to ask a final time if I was sure she should do it. Rising, I opened my palm to her, creating a sheer, shimmering robe of glittering silver snowflakes over her gorgeous, porcelain body.

"Show me what you got, faerie," I encouraged, holding my arm to the side and stepping back.

Sylvie lifted her chin and took in her surroundings before first throwing her left hand out, spirals of her snowy magic twirling through the air but conjuring nothing yet. Smiling, she flicked her right hand now, repeating the action but adding interweaving tendrils of blue. She used her wings to sprint deeper into the woods, and I was quick to follow, still ass naked just the way I preferred.

My mate found a clearing surrounded by thick birch trees as if it were waiting for her to fill the space. She chewed on her bottom lip before poising her hands at the snow-covered ground, spinning circles, ice spreading around her like a skating rink. I folded my arms, watching her unbridled and entirely in her element. Having the opportunity to witness this, her first time using her powers in any way she pleased without fear? Winter's blessing, I must have been the luckiest son of a bitch in the universe.

Once satisfied with the icy ground, she swirled her arms, the blue, white, and shimmering silver magic continuing to coil in ornate patterns. A spiral staircase formed next, followed by several pillars, rising past the tree tops. She ran barefoot for the stairs, her wings flapping excitedly, and ascended the frozen steps. I calmly followed her, taking my time with each stair, watching her tits and ass bounce through that sheer, shimmery fabric as she made her way upward.

When she reached the top, she thrust her hands at the skies, forming a roof over our heads. When she was done, though it was entirely iced over, I could still see the wintry grey clouds and the aurora borealis shimmering in its glorious green, yellow, and pink hues like a magical sky light. Sylvie's arms fell slack at her sides, and her chest heaved. She was breathless and exhausted, but that radiant smile never faded.

"I want to do more, but I think I might pass out if I push it." Sylvie's hands moved to her hips, and she gazed at her handiwork, her eyes glistening with tears.

Appearing behind her, I wrapped my arms around her waist and pressed my cheek to hers. "How do you feel?"

"Free, Jack," she breathed out, leaning against me and letting me support her. "Free."

I tenderly kissed her head and took a moment to gaze at the

icy fortress she'd started. "You know, this may be even more impressive than our actual castle."

Sylvie perked at this, whirling on a heel to face me. "*Our* castle?"

Chuckling, I bopped her nose with a single finger. "Yes. Did you forget the part about you becoming the Winter Queen?"

Sylvie frowned, her hands curling under her chin. "I suppose I did."

"Are you still alright with all of this?" Gently, I rubbed the tip of her ear as she'd done with mine.

She melted against my touch before suddenly burying her face into my chest. "Yes, I just don't know the first thing about being a queen," she confessed, her words muffling against my skin.

Grinning, I curled my arms around her and rested my chin atop her head. "Small steps, Sylvie. You don't have to learn it all in a day or even a month. I've been doing this alone for thousands of years."

"Thank you," she whispered, peeling back to peer at me with those amethyst eyes that still managed to captivate me.

"You know, we could keep coming back here to add onto your creation. Both of us." I took her hand and led her away from the stairs, pulsing magic from my other hand to finish the second ice floor. "We could make it a refuge of sorts. An escape."

Sylvie's eyes brightened as she watched me use my powers. "I'd love that." Her grip tightened against my palm. "But Jack, what about Diedre?"

"We'll deal with her when we have to. I'm still willing to let her have her smaller kingdom if she agrees to leave us the fuck alone, or else I'll banish her to live with the goblins." I clenched my jaw, wishing I could get rid of her entirely at times. She'd have sought *my* demise eons ago if she were able. "I'm certain she'll show up at the most inconvenient time, and when that happens, we'll deal with it. For now, we have your coronation to plan."

Sylvie draped a hand over her face, but still smiled. "Have I told you I loathe being the center of attention?"

"You'd better get used to it, faerie," I teased, tugging her closer. Peeling her fingers from her eyes, I added, "Because the public eye's one thing, but you'll *always* be the center of *my* universe."

Sylvie bit back a sheepish smile, and her cheeks turned rosy. She gasped and slapped a hand on her face. "Jack, I *blushed*. I actually blushed."

"Well, now that you can, I accept this challenge." I grinned wickedly and welcomed her playful slap on my shoulder. "Now then, I'm sure we have a very disgruntled polar bear and stag we left in the cove wondering if we're ever coming back."

Sylvie's eyes widened. "Winter's curse, I feel terrible."

"I'm sure they're fine. I left them in the protection of the ice giant's cave."

"Ice giant?"

Wincing, I snapped my fingers, entirely forgetting there were still so many things Sylvie had yet to learn about winter folk. "Yes, you'll meet him. He's an okay guy, honestly."

"Right," Sylvie answered in a skeptical tone.

I held my hand out to her. "Might I suggest we take a frigid dip into the kingdom's lake as a means of travel back to the Cove?"

Sylvie's wings fluttered. "I thought you'd never ask, mate."

That singular word had my cock twitching, and it didn't go unnoticed by Sylvie, whose gaze snapped straight to it. She arched a mischievous brow.

Despite every bone in my body yearning to fuck my new mate for days on end, the ancient duty in me tethered me back to reality. I held a finger up. "Soon. First, we need our companions back."

"You're such a good king," Sylvie mused, kissing the tip of her finger and touching it to my nose.

Soon, we stood on the lake's edge, its chilly waters lapping at our toes. Sylvie curled against my side, hugging my arm and smiling at the northern lights dancing colorful patterns in the sky.

"Whatever you do, don't let go of my hand, sweetheart. Understand?" With our fingers interlaced, I kissed the back of her hand.

Sylvie wrapped her hand around ours and smiled. "Never."

Twenty-Nine

Sylvie

Fintan and I had never been separated this long. It had my heart thudding against my chest when we approached the cave. An overwhelming impatience to see him, to know he was safe from the previous blizzard, seized me. Jack and I conjured clothes once we reached the lakeshore, and I squeezed his hand to reassure him I wasn't running away.

"Fintan," I shouted, sprinting into the dark cave, turning circles to search for them. There was no one or anything to be found. They were a troupe composed of a huge polar bear, a stag, and a literal frost giant that'd be almost impossible to hide.

"Sylvie," Jack called out. "They're out here." Amusement bounced in his tone with a light chuckle.

Trotting outside, I gasped at the sight of the frost giant rolling a large snowball back and forth with his feet, making Fintan and Nanok chase after it. Fintan paused, leaning forward with his bushy tail poised skyward, wagging. His large, glossy eyes tracked the ball before pouncing on it, clipping the edge with his hoof. Nanok was in a full charge toward the ball, not having enough time to stop, and barreled into Fintan. They both toppled and rolled.

"Fintan," I calmly called out, biting back a smile.

His head popped up, antlers and nose covered in snow, Nanok's dark gaze appearing from the pile beside him. They blinked at us, almost as if confused, before scurrying forward and tackling me and Jack into the snow.

Laughing, I welcomed the outpour of love from my stag and chuckled more when he furiously sniffed me, Jack's polar bear mimicking the same actions beside us. Our scents had changed since completing the mating bond, his icy earthiness mixed now with my sweeter aroma.

Once the animals settled, Jack pushed to his feet, dusting his pants and hair of excess snow, a broad smile plastered to his handsome face. "Thank you for watching out for them, giant."

I'd seen the giant playing with the snowball, but it was another matter entirely when he calmly walked toward us, his gait slower than a sloth. His height challenged the trees, and he sank to one knee, bowing his head at Jack. "It was an honor, your majesty."

My stomach fluttered. I was to be queen. *Jakzair's* queen. The idea of it was still hard to wrap my brain around fully. "Thank you from me as well," I added.

The giant lifted his head, the ice above what would be his eyes shifting upward like arching brows. "Is this her?"

"Yes," Jack replied, his warm smile melting into a gooey one. He held his hand out to me, helping me to stand. "And she's to be made queen very soon."

Everything had transpired so rapidly due to Jack's dwindling timeline. Diedre's curse had robbed us of precious hours, making panic and urgency commonplace. Gasping, I clutched Jack's shirt. "Diedre, we need to do the coronation before she—"

Jack silenced me with a chilly kiss, his full lips gliding over mine, that devilish tongue lapping at mine. "Is it that hard for you to slow down, Sylvie?"

Fintan and Nanok sat next to each other, tilting their heads as if trying to understand our conversation. I glanced at them for answers I knew they couldn't give, but wished they could all the same. "What do you mean?"

"I have time now, Snowflake." Jack clasped his larger hands over mine. "We can stay in the Cove for another three sunsets, the original full timeframe given to me before Diedre's curse. Then we must return to *our* kingdom, where you will be crowned queen. Diedre doesn't possess the power to come here."

Tears filled my eyes because I didn't think I would have the chance to explain to Aella, to Tambie, and the others why my time in the Cove would be shorter now that I would be the Winter Queen. He told me I would never have to say goodbye completely, but I needed to hear it again. To know that Arcane Cove would still always be a second home.

"Jack, tell me again, I'll be able to come back to this place. That I'm not leaving an entire family behind when it comes time." Slipping my arms around his neck, I nervously played with my fingers in his hair.

Jack pinched my chin, keeping my gaze locked with his, and flashed that azure magic in his glacial eyes. "You can come back whenever you wish, Sylvaria. *I'm* the one tied to my kingdom, and it'll be yours by proxy as my mate. As for me, I can only return with you every solstice for a fortnight."

Trailing my hand to the butterfly mark I'd given to him on his forearm, I smiled brightly at his sparkling radiance. "How will I get back?"

Jack pressed a tender kiss to my forehead. "You let me worry about that. For now, I suggest we enjoy what time I have left with your friends."

"My friends? Not yours, too?" I quirked a brow with a tiny smile.

Chuckling, Jack bopped my nose. "Maybe. In time."

Frowning over just being reunited with our animal companions, I stroked Fintan's forehead and between his eyes. "Think everyone will get freaked out if a polar bear strode into the town's center?"

Jack barked a laugh and ruffled Nanok's ears. "Considering the gargoyles, orcs, and minotaur I witnessed and undoubtedly plenty of animal shifters, I highly doubt they'll mind. That is, of course—" He grabbed Nanok's face and pressed his head to his, staring at him. "You don't sniff out any water folk."

My hand clapped to my chest. "My assistant Aegean, he's merfolk."

"Nanok," Jack warned.

The polar bear huffed and lightly bumped his head against Jack's. Jack snickered and scratched underneath his animal's chin. "I'm only kidding. Even if he had a taste for them, they're far harder to catch than lake trout."

"Let's go, then." Curling my arm with Jack's, I shared a leisurely, snowy forest stroll with him to reach the plaza. "Hopefully, Aella hasn't burned down my bakery."

When we arrived in town, only a few townspeople were strolling down sidewalks illuminated by candlelit street lamps in the setting sun. No one paid any mind to us, not even the enormous, fluffy, white bear. We reached the bakery and I petted Fintan's neck, cooing at him, and asking him to wait outside. Faint music fluttered from inside, and strange overlapping scents of sugar, some fruit, and a slight burning smell wafted through the cracks. Sharing a perplexed glance with Jack, I whipped open the door, making the overhanging bell jangle loudly.

Everything appeared in its place in the front room, all appropriately organized on their shelves. The treats in the display case, however, left a little to be desired. What was usually filled with brightly-colored cupcakes, golden brown pastries, and sugar-dusted donuts, now contained—biscuits. Nothing but rows and rows of biscuits that started as burnt to a crisp and gradually got lighter as the display progressed.

Aella appeared from the back room, a mixing bowl in the crook of her arm. "I'm sorry, we're getting ready to change shifts, but—" Her antlers shifted at her forehead when she spotted us, flour smattering her freckled cheeks and nose. "Sylvie," she shouted, throwing the bowl and splattering the counter with some of its contents.

"Miss me?" I teased, holding my arms open wide, ready to receive one of her amazing hugs.

Aella vaulted over the counter and smacked into me, knocking me back on my heels, her arms tightly enveloping me. "I'm so glad you're back. I've quickly discovered that I am not a baker in the slightest."

Wincing from her pinching one of my wings, I patted her back. "I appreciate you trying and watching the shop all the same, friend."

Aella stiffened and pushed me back by my shoulders, her gaze dancing between me and Jack. "Oh my—you two—" A high-pitched squeal that could bring a pack of werewolves to their knees in agony tore from her throat.

Jack shook his pinky in his ear and smiled. "We're mated, yes."

"I'm so, so happy for you," Aella shrieked, hugging me again and then Jack. "Might I say you both look radiant. Like, actually glowing."

Sneaking a peek at Jack, I grinned at his eyes glowing that more vibrant blue, pulsing in time with the butterfly marking. His gaze floated down to my glowing diamond on my chest, and I stroked a finger over it.

The bell over the door chimed, and Aegean appeared with his hands on his hips. "What'd I miss?"

We spent the remaining days in the Cove, visiting with friends who congratulated us on our mate-ship and showered us with affection. Jack appeared surprised, if not taken aback, by how quickly they let him in as one of us. Hopefully, now he has realized why Arcane Cove and its people were so near and dear to my heart.

We shared food and ale as the nights drew near, Jack withstanding the heat from the hearth so long as he kept contact with me. He looked so serene and content to be able to enjoy a warming fire with pleasant company. It made my heart swell knowing I alone could have given that to him.

On our final day, Jack, Aella, Finneas, and several of the children, along with me, made snowmen in the town center. Jack and I were under strict orders not to use our powers, forcing us to make it by hand or the "old-fashioned" way, as Finneas described.

I put off telling Aella that I'd be frequenting the Cove less, making my new kingdom a home as well. A few sobs were shared, but ultimately, she accepted it wasn't a goodbye by any means and teased that she was jealous of the double life I'd get to lead.

I made plans for Aella to run the shop only, and I'd handle the baking, storing things in the fridge as needed, and warming inventory in the stove before selling it or putting it in the display case. Half my time was to be spent in the Cove unless there were pressing matters that needed attending as Winter Queen.

As the final night settled over the magical small town that led me to my mate, I curled my fingers with Jack's, our animal friends at our heels. We slipped into the freezing lake and took the portal home. It was time I accepted the role and responsibilities of Winter Queen, and time we finally *dealt* with Diedre.

Thirty

Sylvie

Jack's castle—our castle—was a wonder of wintry fairy tales. When we emerged from the cerulean lake surrounding it, Nanok and Fintan immediately took the woods, pouncing through the massive snow drifts four times the size the Cove produced. I paused on the bank to take it all in from that vantage point. Nestled within the snow-capped mountains and surrounded by hills of snow and snow-covered evergreens, a glistening white castle stood. Icicles hung from the bottom edges, sparkling when they caught the brightened sun just right. There were two main towers with jutting spires on every side; rounded, elaborate stained glass windows with various shades of blue displayed snowflake designs.

A bridge led to the road from the main iron gate, towering over the lake, and two wide arches were underneath, allowing boats passage. The northern lights danced in vibrant colors in the sky, even during the day, and the lake reflected their radiance.

Tears prickled my eyes, and I gasped when Jack's palm slid against mine. "Jack, it's—" Pausing, I squeezed his hands, fumbling in my mind for the right word. "—breathtaking."

"And now, it's your home, Sylvaria." Jack kissed my cheek while swirling an arm around us, conjuring our outfits from the solstice ball. "Can't have the queen arrive at her castle for the first time naked now, can we?"

Blushing, the new warmth pooled in my cheeks. "If you had *your* way." I arched a wicked brow at my mate.

Jack chuckled and pulled me to his side by my hip. "I'm far too jealous of a male for all that business."

"At least you admit it," I said with a sparkling grin.

Patting my waist, he took my hand and tugged me. "Let me show you where the ceremony will take place and your coronation quarters."

"Coronation quarters?"

Dragging his knuckles lightly over my cheek, he gave me a warm smile like he kept forgetting I didn't come from the same walk of life as him. "It's where you'll bathe, dress, and have your hair and wings prepped."

My wings perked at that before flapping. "My wings?"

"Of course. They deserve to be dolled up like the rest of you for your coronation because much like you—" Jack reached behind me, dragging a finger down the seam separating my wings and making me moan. "—they're gorgeous."

With a grin, I turned to face him, encircling my arms around his neck. "Why don't you make it faster and *take* us there?"

"Whatever you desire, my queen." Jack gave a flash of canine.

My life was already a fairy tale, considering I lived in a magical town full of mystical monsters, creatures, and beings. The Winter Kingdom, I now realized, was my *true* fairy tale, and Jack was my king on a snow-white horse.

In a flurry of snow, we appeared in a vast hallway. Snow piles lined the walls, edging up near each stained-glass window. Crystal chandeliers with hanging beads and gold accents hung between each window. Ornate grey archways hung down the length of the hallway with Nordic scrolling carved into the stone. The floor was shiny azure marble, with the same intricate carvings etched within it.

"Is this where the coronation will be?" Jack let me slip from his grasp, and I turned circles, my skirt twirling with me as I marveled at it.

"No. This would be the main hallway. Hardly a spot for a ceremony." Jack watched me for a beat, folding his muscular arms over his chest, his glacial eyes glinting at the sight of me.

Gliding toward him, I pressed my hands to his chest and beamed. "Show me."

Jack kissed my knuckles and led us through several more hallways. We passed several people, all with the same fae-pointed ears like me and Jack. They were dressed in the same color schemes of white, silver, and pale blue. No one wore the midnight blue of Jack's royal ensemble, and I assumed that shade was reserved for the king alone. The people smiled and whispered to each other, bowing whenever we passed them and returning straight back to chattering.

Leaning closer to Jack, I whispered, "I assume all the chatter surrounds my arrival?"

"Yes, Snowflake. Not only have they never seen a future queen, but also never a winter faerie." Jack trailed his finger around the top edges of one wing, making them vibrate in response.

Stifling a groan from the zing of pleasure swirling in my core from that one fleeting touch, I tightened my grip on his hand. "If you wish me to keep on ceremony, you'd better stop touching my wings like that, *Jakzair*."

"You're right," he responded, pressing his lips to my ear. "That's for later."

His chilly breath, mingling with the minty, snowy scent of him, drew another groan from my throat. All of it whooshed away; no sooner had we stepped into an enormous room. An altar stood at the back, with a dozen white marble stairs leading up to it and a single silver throne at its center. White Corinthian columns circled the throne area, accented with gold. More sapphire-stained-glass windows served as a backdrop, extending to the ceiling. Larger Corinthian columns bordered the room, the leaves at the top interlaced with metallic gold. A swooping archway hung over the stairs at the front of the altar, and the floor was like cerulean glass—transparent and glossy with those same Nordic knot patterns.

"I-I don't know what to say," I breathed out, staring at the ethereal surroundings.

Jack pressed a hand to the small of my back, guiding me forward. "I'm glad you like it. I know there's only one throne, but I wanted to surprise you with yours during the coronation. It'll be right beside mine, both *centered*."

"Surprise me?" I asked, my voice cracking.

Jack brushed a tear that had started to fall down my cheek with his thumb. "I can't thank you enough for making such an important decision so quickly. It would have taken centuries to overcome the ache of losing you after finding you. To know you were out there, and I could never be with you."

"Jack." Tracing my fingers through his beard, I stroked the tip of his ear. He nuzzled his cheek against my palm. "You don't need to thank me. I'm thankful fate brought me to the Cove. I not only got a new family and new friends, but ones who finally accepted me. And best of all?" Rising to my tiptoes to bring our faces closer, I pressed a chaste kiss to his lips. "It brought me my *mate*. Something I never thought I'd ever have."

Jack rested his forehead against mine, his nose drifting through my hair, inhaling me. A guttural growl bubbled in his chest, bits of his ice creature poking through his forehead. The icy cold of it alerted me, and I bit the inside of my cheek to keep from smiling.

"You'd better go get ready for the ceremony, Sylv, before I *and* my creature spark the unrelenting urge to *consummate* this early." Jack rubbed my shoulder, his eyes falling shut, and gulped harshly. He snapped his fingers, and a young woman scurried from the shadows, dressed in a light blue dress with billowing sleeves and silver bordering.

"Yes, m'lord?" She had deep auburn hair that fell to her hips with several braids held together with silver cords. Her hazel eyes lit up when she glanced over to me, grinning as if she already knew what the command would be.

"Take Lady Sylvaria to the coronation chambers and see to it that she's ready by sunset for the ceremony. Her dress and robe should have already been delivered." Jack spoke to the woman, but kept his azure gaze fixed on me.

"Of course, my lord," the handmaiden responded, curtsying. "My lady, will you please follow me?"

"Until sunset? How ever shall I cope being away from you that long?" I flashed him a devious grin.

"I'll make it up to you later tonight," Jack responded, swatting my ass to encourage me to go with the handmaiden.

The handmaiden's cheeks turned rosy, and she nonchalantly itched her nose with a knuckle to hide her smile.

Following beside her, I stretched my wings and continued to take in the palace décor. "My name is Sylvaria, but everyone calls me Sylvie. What's your name?"

"Arryn, my lady." She offered a warm smile and walked with her hands clasped in front of her.

Sunlight now peeked through the stained-glass windows, casting a glittering radiance over the columns, floor, and archways in the hallway.

"Nice to meet you. Do you mind if I ask how long you've been serving the king?"

A tall male fae dressed in a white chef's uniform power-walked past us. There were several brown stains on his shirt, and his expression bordered on terrified. Frowning at this, I opened my mouth to ask Arryn about it, but she spoke first.

"I joined his majesty over twenty winters ago," Arryn answered, undeterred by the panicked chef who'd scurried past.

I glanced over my shoulder at the man picking up speed as he neared a door, but paid it no mind since Arryn didn't seem to think it a big deal. "Twenty? Wow. I guess you know him pretty well, then?

"As much as one could in the very few conversations we've had." Smiling, Arryn opened an opal door with silver accents on our right and ushered me inside. "I'd imagine I don't know him as much as you, my lady."

Arryn has known him for over twenty years. I learned a lot about him in the short time Jack and I had known each other, but it was still unsettling how much there was still to discover.

Pausing at the doorway, I drummed my fingernails on the frame.

"A connection like what Jakzair and I have is a celestial wonder."

Arryn's eyes brightened. "Sounds incredibly romantic."

"Yes." My stomach fluttered at the notion of Jack being my mate, being mine, and soon to be my *king*. "It is."

The room was smaller than the others I'd seen thus far—a cozy, dimly-lit room where the only illumination was orange hues provided by the flames from dozens of candles. A circular white-marbled tub with steaming cerulean water was in the center, facing three windows bordered by grey stone that offered a picturesque view of the snowy mountains. Matching the rest of the castle, stone archways curved toward the ceiling, meeting in the center with Nordic designs carved into every other rock. A mirror bordered with Nordic knots carved out of wood rested to the left of the tub, a basin on a wooden table beneath it. Several towels hung on pegs around the room, and several green fern plants accented the corners.

"If you wouldn't mind removing your clothes. The bath is to temperature already, and I've added milk and lilac." Arryn stuck her finger into the water, swirling it, and nodding when she was satisfied.

This was to be my life now. To go from a winter faerie shunned by my own people, to a bakery owner in a monster town, to the Winter Queen. Life sure loved to keep things interesting, even for an immortal one.

Removing my dress, I looked for a place to set it, but Arryn held out her arms with a grin. Draping the garment over them, I smiled and moved to the tub's edge, the lilac scent wafting from the vapors putting me in a euphoric daze.

"Your wings are beautiful, my lady." Arryn stood at my side, staring at my wings with wide eyes. She tilted her head as I fanned

them, catching the flames' reflection in the crystallized patterns.

"Thank you, Arryn," I responded warmly before dipping my toe into the water. Suppressing a groan at how positively perfect it felt, I shut my eyes and sank until the only thing not submerged was my head.

We spent the better part of an hour chatting and getting to know one another now that she'd be my everyday maiden. I encouraged her to sit on the edge of the tub rather than stand at attention the entire time. Arryn was from a long line of woodland fae and, unfortunately, lost most of her family in a ruthless rebellion war with the sky fae. It left only her and her two younger siblings. To provide for them, she sought employment from the Winter King.

I told her all about my past as well, about Arcane Cove and how Jack's portal finally brought him to me. Arryn remained starry-eyed during the entire story, and only when my fingers began to prune did our conversation end. She helped me into my coronation gown and robes and fastened my jewelry. She pulled bunches of my hair, creating a centerpiece at the back of my head, and making the rest of my hair hang in wavy tendrils. The kingdom's snowflake crest was the final piece, a glittering diamond hairpin she secured on the right side.

When I rose from the chair and stared at my reflection in the mirror, I became a whirlwind of emotions. A part of me hardly recognized myself, whereas another part of me, a sliver buried so deep I hadn't noticed it there before, knew that I was finally seeing *myself* for the first time.

Thirty-One

Jack

Standing in my quarters, I peered at myself in my full-length mirror with an icy silver border. My assistant insisted on helping me into my coronation suit, but as I'd always told him, dressing myself helped me feel normal and would until my reign was over. However, it wasn't as if that day would ever come. And that was fine—*more* than fine now that I found Sylvie. I no longer dreaded spending the rest of eternity *alone*.

I adjusted the pearlescent cufflinks on each end of my jacket. This would be the first and last time the kingdom would see a ceremony such as this. I'd performed countless knighting ceremonies over the centuries, but never placed a crown on a woman's head, declaring her my mate and queen.

Per tradition, I wouldn't see her again until she strode the royal blue carpet toward me, waiting for her by our thrones. An icy chill wrenched my spine from the separation. What if she were nervous? I wanted to calm her. What if she was scared? I wanted to rid her of *any* possible fears. Instead, I continued to check my white over-jacket, plucking any exposed stray threads from the golden filigree embroidery. Faux fur draped over each of my shoulders, and the shirt beneath was sewn from the same lake's frozen waters, trapped with magic and starlight.

My assistant, Rathal, carried my cloak, its weight already making me dread having it placed on my shoulders. He slung it over my back, and I winced at how heavy it was over my arms.

Groaning, I stretched my back and adjusted the cloak, making it lie evenly across my shoulders. "This godsdamned thing is always so heavy and *hot*."

Though once I had my mate's hand in mine, the heat of it wouldn't matter as much.

"Sorry, my lord. You can most certainly whip it off for the after-party. Kingly duties and all that." Rathal shifted some of his short, midnight black hair over one pointed, pale ear. He offered a meager smile, his brown gaze dropping to the cloak to fuss over it some more.

"Oh, can I? Thank you so much for the permission, Rath." A much-needed chuckle bounced from my throat.

Rathal was one of my best friends, and though he was my assistant, I never saw him as a servant by any means. I told him long ago he didn't have to stand on ceremony when it was just us. Thankfully, it only took me three times of saying it before he acquiesced. It was the only bit of normalcy I got to experience, and I cherished every moment of it.

Rathal smoothed out my hair on the sides and gave a curt nod. "I'm not sure how much more perfect you can look."

Slowly swiveling on my heel, I raised a brow at him. "Whoa, what are you after? Complimenting my appearance today? I seem to recall you fearing my head would explode?"

Rathal smirked and turned for a cabinet on the far wall. "It *is* a special occasion and one that won't happen again. Call it a grace."

Leave it to an old friend to make an excitedly nerve-wracking situation feel more like an average day in the palace. Sweat had already started to bead at the base of my neck and across my forehead. I couldn't have my mate's hand in mine soon enough.

Rathal returned, holding my crown in both hands. He raised it to my head, discreetly positioning it and careful not to dishevel my hair in the process. I focused on the giant sapphire mounted at the center, its shape and color like the lake's portal.

"It's time, my lord," Rathal announced, pulling me from my daze. He stood at the open door with his hand folded behind his back.

After taking one final glance at myself in the mirror, the last time I'd see the reflection of a lonely king seemingly doomed to shoulder the burdens alone, I smiled and followed Rathal to the throne room.

More than a hundred fae lined each side of the blue carpet. They chattered and bounced on their heels, repeatedly looking for Sylvie's entrance. They went silent once Rathal announced my arrival. As I strode through the gauntlet of my people, each curtsied or bowed. On the altar, the queen's new throne rested *directly* next to mine.

It was customary for the king to be seated when the queen took the walk toward the altar to be crowned. Fuck sitting. Sylvaria wasn't just a queen; she was my mate, my life's breath, and she *rescued* me. Standing at the ready for her was the least I could offer.

"Presenting, the Lady Sylvaria," they announced, and the room went as silent as newly fallen snow.

Sylvie, with Arryn in tow, carrying her train, took her first steps across the blue carpet. Jaws dropped, eyes bulged, and smiles blazed with every person she passed. That amethyst gaze didn't look at any of them because her focus stayed on me. Her dress was pure white, metallic silver threading weaving tree branches over the cinched bodice and full skirt. A matching faux fur cloak adorned her shoulders.

A wide smile graced Sylvie's lips once she reached me.

Leaning toward her, I whispered, "You look *resplendent*."

The grin hadn't faded from her lips. "Such a big word. I'm flattered."

Smirking, I gestured to her on where to stand at my side. Arryn fixed her train, resting it perfectly, before joining the crowd. Sylvie bowed her head to me, and I immediately rested my knuckle under her chin, stopping her.

"No need for that, Snowflake. You'll never have to bow to me. You are my *equal* even before the crown rests on your head." I traced my thumb over her jawline, sniffing from the burning sensation in my nose.

Tears built in Sylvie's eyes, and she yanked one white satin glove off, handing it to Arryn, who scurried to retrieve it. Sylvie took my hand in hers and pressed our palms tightly together. "I'm ready, Jack."

"This will be quick," I assured her, kissing the corner of her brow.

Turning to the awaiting crowd, I slid on the proverbial royal mask. "People of Winter, I gathered you all here today for what will become one of the kingdom's grandest of celebrations."

Sylvie's hammering pulse vibrated against our clenched palms.

"The Winter Kingdom, after over a thousand years without, will finally have its long-awaited queen," I announced, my voice booming from the marble walls.

The crowd roared with whistles, claps, and overwhelming shouts of joy. Sylvie's cheeks flushed a rosy tint, her throat bobbing as she gulped. I stared at her profile, the pride and determination dancing in her gaze as she surveyed an atrium of fae soon to be *her* people, and my chest ached. Silver charms decorated each of the top corners of her forewings—two thin silver chains draped from charm to charm like a winged necklace.

Slipping my hand from hers only long enough to grab the scepter and crown resting on her throne, I returned to Sylvie and rested the scepter in her arms. Hiding the crown behind me, I gestured at her. "I present to you, the Lady Sylvaria, whom I not only accept as our reigning Winter Queen, but who has also become my eternal mate."

The cheers at that were deafening to the point I couldn't hear my own thoughts.

"Sylvaria," I beckoned, holding her crown out to her and reveling at the gasp that fell from her throat.

With a trembling hand, she reached for it, almost fearful of touching it. "Jack, that's absolutely beautiful."

"It's crafted uniquely for you. The crystals are from our kingdom's mountains, and captured snow makes the silver metal sparkle." Raising it, I caught the sun's rays piercing through the stained glass, making the crystals sparkle. "My queen," I whispered before resting the crown atop her head.

"All hail Queen Sylvaria," a squire shouted. "Long may she reign."

Roars of "hail" echoed through the space.

"And hail King Jakzair," the squire added, the excited applause growing louder.

Turning Sylvie toward me, I cupped her face with both hands and swirled patterns on her cheeks. "From being cast out to now being a part of *two* homes, my sweet Sylvie." I pressed a light kiss to her lips, quickly swiping away an escaped tear from her cheek.

Sylvie sniffled and dabbed her eyes with a knuckle. She peered over my shoulder and stifled a laugh. "I think we have two disgruntled animals that weren't invited to the ceremony."

Behind me, Nanok and Fintan had their large, black noses shoved against the window, fogging it up. "I'll have them brought in for the party."

"Party?" Sylvie's face brightened.

Grinning, I ran the tip of one of her ears between my fingers. "You really haven't been around fae folk in a while, have you?"

A light moan resonated in her throat from my touch, her eyes closing. "You know the answer to that, Jack."

"Well, my dear faerie," I started, leading her to the thrones. "Of course, there will be a party. We look for *any* excuses for festivities."

Sylvie clapped a hand to her chest and pointed at her new throne. "Is this mine?"

"Yes," I whispered, kissing against her hair and inhaling her sweet aroma. "Why don't you try it out?"

Sylvie's spine straightened. She circled the air in front of the throne with her finger. "As in, sit on it? Something so perfect and pretty?"

Cupping her elbows, I flashed a smug grin. "Much like I intend on you sitting on my face soon."

Her cheeks heated, and she nudged the butt of the scepter into my ribs.

I stroked a hand over my beard and idly shrugged, still donning the same smile.

Sylvie's eyes rolled adorably. She turned on her heel, slowly sinking until she sat on the throne's edge. After a few beats, she slid back and rested her arms. "I didn't expect it to be this comfortable."

"All in the craftsmanship." I trailed my gaze over the way she complemented the throne—its design similar to mine with blues, silvers, and whites, wintry accents of snowflakes and icicles. Sylvaria's, however, had a flared pair of icy wings that I carved myself.

Sitting on my throne to her left, I kept our hands locked together, and side by side we gazed at our kingdom's people. They chittered, pointed, and shouted jovially toward us, antsy to let their excitement out through dancing and merriment. Leaning toward Sylvie, I brought her hand to my lips and trailed feathered kisses over her knuckles. "Would you care to announce the festivities?"

"What do I say?" Sylvie pinched her lips together, gaze shifting from the growing, raucous crowd and back to me.

"Whatever comes to mind. They'll get the idea rather quickly, I assure you."

Sylvie rose, something I hadn't been expecting. I raised a brow at her, but she gave me a reassuring smile. "People of Winter," she started, waiting for them to quiet down like a seasoned royal professional. "I'm honored to be called your new queen. Now that the formal matters are past us, let's eat, drink, and dance until sunrise or until slumber finds us, whichever comes first."

The crowd went into joyful hysterics over my gorgeous queen's choice of words. When Sylvie sat down, I was leaning back in a corner of my throne, my elbow propped on an armrest, and gawking at her. "I think you're going to be just fine, faerie."

With a deviously sweet smile, Sylvie rested the scepter on her seat and stretched over the chairs to kiss me. "Why don't you take off that cloak and come dance with me?"

"You'll never have to ask me twice, Sylv." Rising and undoing the clasp that held my cloak in the same breath, I let it pile in a heap on my throne. I pressed a hand to her lower back and pulled her closer. "I'll dance naked on top of a frozen lake if you ask me."

Sylvie traced the snowflake kingdom crest on my shirt. "Oh, yeah? What about at the peak of a volcano?" Her grin was downright foxy.

"Now you're not playing fair." After giving the corner of her lips a peck, I led her from the altar and to the awaiting dancefloor, where couples already twirled circles around one another.

Several guards escorted Nanok and Fintan into the throne room despite their reservations about having animals inside the castle. Nanok was immediately on the hunt for food, while Fintan searched for Sylvie, content to roam the space when he'd found her and received some good head scratches.

Rathan brought us silver goblets filled to the brim with red cranberry wine. Sylvie was quick to grab one, sipping on it and humming over how sweet and delicious it tasted. I arched a brow at how quickly she finished it, beckoning for another. Sipping from my glass, I chuckled into the goblet, my laughter echoing against the metal.

Sylvie was on her second gulp of fresh wine when she paused and squinted at me. "What's so funny?"

"I suppose I should've warned you about fae wine when you're not used to it."

Sylvie gazed into her cup with the most adorable little pout.

"But then I realized there's no danger with you throwing your inhibitions out the fucking door now and again, is there?" Pulling her closer, I nuzzled my nose against her temple. "And you're always safe with me, Sylvaria."

"Mm," she cooed into my neck, her fingers playing in my hair. "Then twirl me until you're the only thing keeping me standing."

Laughing, I obliged her request, waltzing us in unruly circles between others twirling on the dancefloor. Sylvaria let her head fall back, giggling, some of the wine in her goblet splashing to the floor. The lively music melted into a slower, seductive pace as the violin in the band took center stage.

Sylvaria caught my gaze, bringing her wine to my lips and encouraging me to drink. Flashing my fangs at her, I slipped the cup from her grasp and downed it, handing it off to the first tray that passed. "You're *so* fucking handsome, Jack."

Pulling her tighter, I dipped my pinky into the low back of her dress and pressed my forehead to hers. "I know."

"Frosty, you son of a—" Sylvie cackled, her joyous laughter rivaling the music.

Capturing her mouth with mine, I slow-danced us in circles, my fingers massaging the back of her neck and tangling in her pale, wavy hair. The wine's effects buzzed in the back of my head, and I slunk from the dancefloor, yanking Sylvie into the darkened area behind the thrones. There was just enough space between the altar and the wall for us to fit, facing each other.

"What's this? The king sneaking away during such a prestigious ceremony?" Sylvie teased, nibbling her bottom lip and looping her fingers in my belt loops.

Pressing the hardened thickness straining in my pants against her stomach, I placed my hands against the wall above her head.

"I couldn't fucking help myself. I was right, by the way."

Sylvie unabashedly palmed my erection, squeezing the fabric. "About what?"

"What a queen you would make," I whispered, my voice gravelly. The crown complemented her hair, her glowing, lilac eyes, her high cheekbones, but most of all, it suited *her*.

Sylvie smiled at me, bright and full of vigor, before whimpering. She crashed her mouth to mine, her fevered motions knocking my crown from my head. I caught it before it hit the marble floor, holding it at my side. My free hand teased tantalizing circles over her wings against the wall. We were two teenagers who snuck away to make out in a broom closet in that moment.

Fucking winter's curse. *I* was the first one to pull away. Panting, I ran my thumb over the smeared lipstick staining Sylvie's mouth, smoothing it out. "We should get back to the party, Snowflake."

Sylvie pouted and shoved her forehead against my chest. "I suppose you're right yet again."

Chuckling, I stroked her hair. "We have all night, my mate."

"I'm holding you to that—" Sylvie started, gripping my cock through my pants again. "—your *majesty*."

"Promises, promises," I mused, nudging my head for her to move first.

Wickedly shimmying past me, making sure her tits brushed my ribs, she waved at me before thrusting her fists in the air when in view of the crowd. "Who wants more wine?"

Shaking my head, I speared a hand through my hair, straightening it before resting the crown on my head. When I appeared from behind the altar, Rathan stood in the crowd with his arms folded and a knowing, sardonic grin playing on his lips.

I shrugged at him.

The night carried on with two more casks of wine opening, the dancing becoming far more chaotic and messier. Sylvie had grabbed the attention of our lead chef, interested in how he made certain dishes, before offering her own advice. Nanok and Fintan received enough attention to last them several lifetimes. And me? I was content to prop myself on a wall and observe it all, let it sink in what a lucky bastard I was and how this night could not have been more perfect.

The sudden dull scent of sulfur hanging in the air had my shoulders tensing. There were several firelit lamps and endless candles, but that particular smell put me on full alert. Nanok's head poked above the crowd, his nose sniffing the air. Our shared wintry glow radiated in his eyes, his teeth baring in a protective snarl.

A plume of grey smoke and spiraling, inky black tendrils appeared in the middle of the dance floor, a shadowy figure materializing a moment later with a blade poised at one of my guards' necks. I'd prepared for it. Only it was impossible to guess *when* it would happen. Stepping in front of my mate, my palms poised in front of me, I readied to deal with the Snow Queen once and for all.

Thirty-Two

Sylvie

One moment, I was deliriously happy and tipsy on fae wine, and in the next, I'd immediately sobered at the sight of *Diedre*.

When the room fell silent and all matters of celebration ceased, Diedre clacked her teeth. "Oh, by all means, don't stop the party on my account."

Throwing my hands out, I launched icy walls down the length of the carpet, shielding everyone in attendance within them.

Jack was quick to coax me behind him. Nanok and Fintan barreled through the crowd. Nanok growled, the fur along his spine bristling. Fintan scraped his hooves, his antlers poised for attack.

"You call off those animals, or not only does the guard get his throat sliced, but I'll make bear jerky and glue out of those two." Diedre pinched the dagger closer to the guard's neck, making him whimper and bleed slightly.

We gave our animals calming gestures to stay put, and I folded my wings defensively at my back.

"Diedre, I half expected you to crash the ceremony right as I was to put the crown on Sylvie's head. How thoughtful of you to *wait*,"

Jack said through gritted teeth, holding me to his side tighter.

Diedre shrugged one shoulder. "I would've come sooner, but you keep quite the defenses up. It took me some time to break through the shielding spells. What sorcerers do you employ anyway, Jakzair?"

"As if I'd tell you." Jack gripped my waist before stepping closer to Diedre. She tensed, the elbow holding the blade poised higher. "I'm going to ask you one final time, Diedre. I've been gracious to you, and there are far too many people I care about at risk now that I've run out of patience with you."

Diedre's glossy black eyes narrowed. "Ask me *what?*"

"Are you going to be a *problem?*" Jack's commanding voice was like thunder rattling the rafters, his ice creature poking through his face, the accompanying lightning strike.

Diedre's resolve wavered when the ice monster started to reveal itself. She backed away, taking the guard with her. "I will never stop going after what should have rightfully been mine."

Jack sighed, his right hand turning into crystallized magic. "Then I hereby revoke your kingdom, Diedre."

His words were met with such shock and animosity that Diedre let the blade fall away from the guard's neck. "You can't do that. You don't have the right, nor the power."

Taking the small window of opportunity, I curled my magic around the guard's torso, tugging him toward me and ushering him behind the shield wall.

"You're right, I didn't when you *cursed* me." Jack lifted his icy fist, frosty vapors misting from it. "But now that it's lifted—" His eyes glowed, the creature taking them over until they became icy hot.

"No, no. All I ever wanted was my birthright. You were *created* to ensure I never got the throne." Diedre spoke with venom dripping from her tongue, the black liquid that never ceased leaking from her eyes streaking her cheeks and dripping to the floor.

"Well, it's a good thing destiny has its way of working things out. You spoiled your chances with this kingdom the day you succumbed to the darkness." Jack thrust his arm forward, aiming his open hand at Diedre. "I'm banishing you to that very darkness you hold dear."

Diedre's eyes went wide, her fists shaking violently at her sides. "No. I will never let you live this down, Jakzair. Do you hear me?"

"You are hereby banished to the Outerwoods and stripped of your kingdom on the mainland. Though I can't take away your title, perhaps you could become—" Jack smirked, his wrist twisting, fingers curling. "—queen of the goblins."

Diedre set her jaw tight and lifted her chin, her gaze roaming the throne room of fae folk, peeking over the icy walls.

"Any last words?" Jack asked.

Diedre clicked her long, pointy, onyx nails together. "It may take me a thousand years to conjure a spell, *King* Jakzair—" She paused, her soulless eyes darting to me now. "—but I *will* find a way to get my revenge."

Glaring at her, I flared my wings, lightly flapping them to show Diedre I wasn't afraid of her.

"Then I guess we have a thousand years to make our wards impenetrable. Have a nice life, Diedre." Jack snapped his fingers, and she vanished with a wailing shriek.

Launching for my mate, I wrapped my arms around him, holding him tight. "Jack."

"She left me no choice, Sylvie. I gave her every possible

opportunity," he mumbled against my neck.

I peeled back and searched his half-icy face. "I know. She was a threat to the kingdom, its people, to me, and our animals. All of it. You did the right thing."

"I'm not sure I could ever convey to you in words how much that means to me. How much finding *you* means to me." Jack rested a hand on my nape, his shoulders sinking from the effort with Diedre.

"Then make this royal affair official and *show* me how much, Jakzair." Rising to my toes, I kissed him—deeply, profoundly, and with so much heat behind it that it melted the walls I created as shields for our people.

Jack's arm curled around me, bending me backward with his own passion that he poured into that kiss. He grunted, pointing at someone, then to our animals for him to tend to them. In a shimmer of snow, we appeared in a massive bedroom, my back flopping onto the oversized kingly bed, ice-blue satin soft against my skin.

Jack's mouth was still pressed to my lips, his tongue diving in to swirl with mine. I dug my fingers into his hair, gripping it, tugging it, before slipping a hand to his pants and greedily pulling at the belt.

Jack snatched my wrists and pulled away, gazing down at me hungrily, like a lion who'd caught his prey. "Considering we're not in any rush, there are matters I need to attend to that got neglected."

A flutter whooshed through my core, surging to my clit and making it throb. Jack trailed his touch between my breasts, dragging over my stomach, and at the center of my hips. The dress misted away in mystical spirals of snow and iridescent sparkles as he went. Jack tugged my hips, inciting me to open my eyes and look at him. The creature still played in his gaze, the ice forming over his forehead. When he smiled, those devious canines extended, and the long, dark blue tongue flicked out.

Winter's blessing.

The rest of him remained in his fae form, and he swirled that tongue around my navel, flicking it from one hipbone to the other. He curled his arms behind my thighs and hoisted my ass from the bed, bringing my pussy within an inch of his mouth. His icy breath pooled over the sensitive flesh there, and I gripped the sheets, already crying out from the sensation. And then Jack *licked*. One torturously slow lap of his tongue over my center, the coolness of it seeping into my skin and giving me a euphoric shiver.

Jack licked several more times from top to bottom, pausing only long enough to suck on my clit and making me scream. Pulling his tongue back into his mouth, he kissed my inner thigh and smiled against it, grazing one of his fangs over my skin.

"Do you want more, faerie?" Jack's monster surrounded those words, gravelly and deep, but it was still entirely him. Both sides of him had always been him, and now it felt like a union between all of us.

Panting, I sat up on my elbows. "Yes," I growled out, imagining if I had my own inner monster what she'd sound like.

Jack pushed me back to the bed with a firm hand on my chest. My wings fanned out, cradling me as I nestled into the duvet again. Jack plunged his tongue inside me. I tensed, gasped, and my back arched from the bed. It was wet, it was cold, and it moved inside me so erotically I couldn't think straight. It twisted, writhed, licked, and when it reached that sweet spot deep inside, it *flicked* there repeatedly. Jack had pushed his tongue so far in that his lips met my center, morphing from his softer fae mouth to his colder, harder creature.

Everything altogether was so overwhelming, I writhed on the bed, my knees trying to hitch, my hips attempting to rotate side to side. But Jack held onto me, not allowing me to do any of it as he ate me out like a snow cone covered with the elixir of fucking life. Flick. Flick. My muscles were already tightening, the release building, but when Jack tipped his nose to my clit, rubbing there with it, I came completely undone, screaming into the rafters.

Jack slowly slid his tongue out and kissed each of my thighs, a smug grin still poised on his lips. "I saw the way you looked at my creature's tongue that day, Snowflake. How could I possibly not give you precisely what you desired?"

An icy sheen of sweat coated my body and face. Laughing from the barrage of endorphins rocketing through my veins, I sat up enough to curl a hand around Jack's neck and pulled him on top of me. "Finish the ceremony, Jack. I need you inside me." Clutching his shirt, I made his clothes disappear in the same fashion he made mine.

Flashing one canine, Jack positioned himself between my thighs. While he kissed me, he used one leg to hitch under my knee, spreading me wider for him. The tip of him teased my entrance, and as slow as a melting iceberg, pushed himself inside. He'd done it this way when he took my virginity so that I didn't endure any pain. This time, he did it so we could savor the moment, because now we *could*.

He pulled away from the kiss, staring down at me and sharing the same breaths with me. In and out he rocked, slow and delicious enough to make me quiver, my nails digging into his back. My winged mark on his arm glittered and pulsed, making the sensations more pronounced. Jack was my mate, my husband, and now I was his *queen*.

Jack pressed a light kiss to my forehead, his fingers grazing my hair. "Sit up for me." With his hand guiding my back, we sat facing each other, him still buried deep inside.

His rock-hard muscles were on full display without the icy ridges of his creature. I played my fingers over his abs, traced the underside of each pec, and squeezed his bicep. Jack pressed a hand to my ass and guided me forward and back, encouraging me to rock myself over him.

"Tell me, faerie," Jack started, reaching for one of my wings. He gave a feathery touch to the top, making me shiver, and moved it toward the center of the forewing. "Which part is the most sensitive?"

Sucking in a shaky breath, I swallowed and answered, "The central point between them. Right at my—" Before I finished, Jack found the spot, his fingers grazing up and down over my spine.

I clenched around his cock, the sensations from his touch on my wings making me see stars behind my eyelids. No one had ever touched me there. For faeries, it was more intimate than even our breasts. It led to a nerve ending that traveled nearly the entire length of our torso, including where Jack was buried now.

"Too much?" Jack asked, still lightly stroking behind my wings.

Wrapping an arm around him for leverage, I bucked on and off him, making our hips slap together with each stroke. "Keep doing it, Jack," I whispered, my head lulling back from the electricity sparking beneath my skin.

Jack lowered his lips to my nape and grazed his fangs over my skin, nibbling and sucking. We worked in tandem now, thrust for thrust. His hand tantalized my wings, and I dug my nails into his back, scratching him because I damn well couldn't help myself. Jack sank his teeth into me, but not as deeply as when he claimed me. This time was for pure pleasure and *fun*. My insides quivered around him, a surge I had never experienced building within my core. When it went taut, my magic burst from my hands and mouth, filling the room. Jack growled against my throat and released inside me in icy hot spurts that prolonged my orgasm.

Jack chuckled, light and carefree. "You're a marvel, Syl." His lips pressed to mine. "And clearly, you want every room to look like your ice castle."

My eyes flew open and panned the bedroom. Ice coated the floor, the ceiling, the chandeliers—everything had been frozen. "This is exactly why they were afraid of me. I'm unpredictable, I—"

Jack shut me up with a kiss, his hand kneading at my jaw. "Sylvaria, my queen, my mate, my eternal love, you've done nothing but turn our room into ice. Nothing. You are *not* a danger here."

My eternal love.

Tears blurred my vision, and I pressed a hand to his chest, feeling his thrumming heartbeat against my palm. Heat pooled against my skin. Not icy warmth like everything else Jack exuded, but actual *heat*. "Jack, your heart."

A knowing, cocky smile quirked Jack's lips. He brought my hand to his mouth, kissing my knuckles. "Only for you, Snowflake."

I'd come a long way from the faerie lands buried deep in the Norwegian mountains. Arcane Cove found me, and with it came lifelong friends who understood me and accepted me. Now, because of a magical small town, I'm forever bonded with my mate, and I *melted* Jack Frost's icy heart.

Epilogue

Sylvie

A year later...

"Aella," I shouted, shimmying from the bakery's backroom with my tenth tray of sugar cookies. "How are they doing with the decorating out there?"

Aella threw her hands to her hips and shook a chastising finger at me. "Sylvie, what did I say? They've got it handled. You take several deep breaths and concentrate on these cookies, yeah?"

"Right. Yes," I breathed out, grabbing the blue and white icing dispensers.

Aella sidled behind me and hugged my shoulders. "It's going to be perfect, Syl. And even if it isn't, do you really think he'll care?"

I'd spent the last year living a glorious double life. Some days would be spent in the Winter Kingdom, handling royal decrees with Jack, paying visits to surrounding towns, and holding festivals within the palace walls to celebrate occasions with fellow fae folk. Other days, I'd travel through the mirrored portals the kingdom sorcerers created for me that led *only* to Arcane

Cove. The portal would appear only to me, and no one else, a stipulation I insisted on to keep the Cove safe, just in case anyone managed to sneak into our chambers. The latter was unlikely, but I'd never forgive myself if it were my fault something bad made its way through.

Aella was always waiting for me on the other side, excitedly jumping and wrapping me in one of her world's best hugs. We spent the rest of that day baking, and I taught her everything I knew. Aegean had picked up a lot as well in the past year since I asked him to bake more when the supply I created started to run low. Everything worked like a well-oiled machine, and I got to spend much-needed personal time in my element. It was nice being able to see my friends still, to pull up a stool and grab a drink at Finneas', or eat some tasty lunch at the Minty Boar with Aella, and catch up. The ache that would start to form in my chest at Jack's absence, however, had me usually returning to the kingdom within a couple of days. It was like leaving a sliver of my soul behind.

Today, the winter solstice has approached. Today would be different. Jack would be here. He could be here in the Cove *with* me for *two* whole weeks. It stood to reason that I was equally as nervous as I was excited. This would be the first time we could spend moments in my first true home without worrying that Diedre would ruin it. There'd be no rushing, and we had already been mated for an entire year. There'd be no tip-toeing around that particular elephant in the room either.

"You're right. He won't care, but that still doesn't mean I don't want to try and make it the best welcoming party I can." Smiling at my maenad friend, I decorated the snowflake-shaped cookies with the blue and white icing before sprinkling my magic over them. The clock chimed overhead, and I yelped, scurrying the trays onto my arms and dashing for the door.

Aella sprinted past me to open it, saluting one of her small antlers as I grinned at her in gratitude. "I know you're not thinking straight, and I can't blame you. Your mate is *hot*."

Laughing, I placed the cookies on the display table with the other treats—wintry cupcakes, sugar-dusted blueberry-filled donuts, blue sugar crystals on a stick, blueberry muffins, and chocolate cupcakes with tiny snowmen on top. I made the last one as a bit of an inside joke with Jack, making the body out of vanilla swirled icing, a marshmallow for the head with chocolate eyes and mouth, orange icing for the carrot nose, and two small pretzel sticks as its arms.

"Come on, everyone. We'll meet him at the lakeshore. He's going to be so surprised you're all there." Bouncing on my heels, I clapped my hands together and started to walk. My pace picked up to a sprint, which led into full flight mode, my wings fluttering excitedly.

"Want me to give you a ride?" I heard Vorthak say.

"You're out of your damn mind if you think I'm letting you carry me," Dagnar answered, Tambie's all-telling giggle following.

"Suit yourself," Vorthak answered, his large wings flapping.

Fintan met me halfway through the woods, galloping beside me and huffing into the chilly wind, making spiral vapors from his breath. The first snow had yet to fall, the trees having lost most of their leaves, and the grass was a dull brown.

I smoothed a hand over his head. "Daddy's coming, Fintan."

And winter came with him.

My heart was racing by the time I made it to the lake. My eyes stung from the wind blowing in during flight, tears blurring my vision. In the distance, the lake began to freeze over steadily, the pace increasing, the faint sight of two sets of bubbles edging closer.

When Jack's head emerged, followed by Nanok's, my breath hitched in my throat. Those glowing, glacial eyes peeked out next, the skin at the corners crinkling because he was already smiling at the sight of me. The rest of him appeared bit by bit as he ascended from the water—his bulky shoulders, carved pecs, that dangerous six-pack of abs, the light blonde happy trail leading to his—

"Sylvie, what in the name of the goddess?" Finneas barked behind me.

Biting my lip, I innocently turned to a group of five shocked townsfolk.

Finneas had his hand over his eyes. "You didn't say he was going to be butt ass naked."

"I certainly don't mind," Tambie added, tilting her head to one side.

Dionysus' gaze dropped to Jack's lower half, and he glared at it before teasingly throwing his hand over Chelsea's eyes. "Oh no, you don't, Red."

Vorthak slowly cocooned himself with his massive wings and grumbled. "Let me know when he's got some damn clothes on."

"What's all this?" Jack asked, coming up beside me and *still* naked.

My cheeks warmed as I turned to face him. "Surprise," I said, without as much preamble as I'd hoped for.

"Did you forget I preferred to make the swim without clothes? Less friction?" Jack grinned, flashing those delicious canines.

Clearing my throat, I curled my hair behind my ears. "Yes. Yes, I did. Otherwise, I would've advised everyone to wait at the town center."

Nanok shoved his head under my arm, demanding I pet him. After he was satisfied with my efforts, he tackled Fintan.

Sparkling, snowy spirals traveled up Jack's body, starting at his feet. A pair of jeans and a light blue V-neck shirt appeared on him, the snowflake charm bouncing into place. "What's in the town center?"

Tambie elbowed Finneas and Vorthak in the sides. "You two oafs can look now."

I slapped a hand on my forehead. None of this was going as planned, and I wanted to whine like a child. "I wanted this all to be a surprise. To lure you there, and everyone be all like, surprise," I made deflated jazz hands in the air between us.

Jack cupped my face and circled his thumbs over my cheeks. He bent to kiss me, and the devious slide of his tongue between my lips had my knees buckling. "I *am* surprised. And I still haven't seen the town center. Show me." His eyes glinted as he smiled, his gaze lifting to everyone behind me and waving at them. "Hello, everyone. Good to see you again."

"Great to see *you* too, Jack," Tambie answered, swiveling her hips.

When we emerged from the woods to the town's center, the solstice tree was already up, littered with dozens of snowflake ornaments crafted by the town's children. I used my magic to create an ice rink where an ogre boy and a demon boy were currently skating circles and falling on their butts, laughing. There were four large tables filled with the wintry-themed desserts, and a giant lighted banner hung from one flamelit lamp post to the other: "Welcome Home, Jack."

"Sylvie, you did all of this? For me?" Jack's lips parted, and he stared in awe at the display.

Everyone clapped and hollered, repeatedly yelling surprise.

"Of course I did, Jack." Using my wings to float in front of him so I didn't have to rise on my toes, I curled my arms around his neck and kissed him. "Arcane Cove brought us together, and you are just as much a member of this community as any of us."

"Thank you," Jack whispered, holding me in his arms. He turned to everyone else and held up a hand. "Thank you to everyone."

"One more thing," the mayor Tiberius said, his taloned feet clacking against the cobblestones as he made his way toward us. His scaled tail swished, kicking up dirt, and he held out a giant, shimmering white key. "I know you can't stay here for an extended amount of time, but also know you would if you could. She's right, you should feel like a Cove citizen. For that, I give you a key to the city."

Jack took it and bowed his head. "I'm honored."

More whoops and hollers followed, Finneas clapping the loudest.

"If this is a welcoming party for the Winter King, it's missing something," Jack said, grinning at me.

I frowned, looking around at what I could have possibly missed. A giant snowflake landed on the tip of my nose, followed by dozens more, absolutely flooding the skies.

"It's snowing," the ogre child cried out excitedly.

"Already?" Herb said gruffly, adjusting his belt.

Vorthak laughed and clapped him on the back. "Don't be such an old fart."

"I *am* an old fart."

Still floating with my wings, Jack pulled me closer, wrapping his arms around my ass. Bits of his creature poked through his face, a more natural and welcoming occurrence for him after we were mated. He grinned at me with those pearly fangs, and warmth coiled in my belly. Pressing my hands to his cheeks, I kissed the icy ridges protruding from his forehead. "Welcome home, Jack *Frost*."

And with the snow falling in troves, neither of us bothering to use magic to shield it from collecting on our clothes or hair, Jack playfully *nipped* at my nose.

STAY TUNED FOR BOOK 3 IN

Scan the QR Code Below to Check Out More of my Works!

@authorcarlyspade on all social media

linktr.ee/authorcarlyspade

STAY TUNED!

WWW.CARLYSPADE.COM

Books by Carly Spade

Thus far, he's avoided capture, until a mysterious beauty sneaks onto his ship, ensnaring him with her cunning nature. What starts as a devious plan to use her for his own gain blossoms into mythical discoveries and a journey into territory he never dreamed of crossing—a devotion far deeper than to the sea herself.

An adult pirate romantasy Calico Jack x Anne Bonny historical reimagining.

BUY IT ON AMAZON

Acknowledgments

Initially, the idea for this book spawned from my desire to create a new version of Jack Frost that has never been seen before. Then, it blossomed into a ship that was popular when *Rise of the Guardians* was out some years ago between Jack Frost and Elsa from *Frozen*. So, this book is for anyone who may have ever fantasized about a beefier Jack with tattoos and a beard, or anyone who ever supported that ship but make her a Faerie baker. 😊

Thank you to my critique partner, AK for staying honest with me and telling me when something truly isn't working and saying, "You can do better." Your belief in me keeps me going, keeps me confident, and reminds me that yes, I *can* do better. It's taken some time during my two-year lurch but I feel this book has truly brought me back and I have you to thank for that as well.

Thank you, Cerys, for not only alpha reading this book once, but one and a half times as I re-vamped the beginning of the story to the best of my ability. Your enthusiasm for my work and continued willingness to squeal and fangirl about ideas as I bounce them off you has remained a detrimental part of my author journey.

Thank you to the artists that have created gorgeous art pieces of both Jack, Sylvie, Nanok, and Fintan before and during my drafting process. These inspired me greatly to make the story live up to the artwork and if you're reading this and haven't seen them go to my social media accounts right meow and look for them! They're stunning and created by HUMANS.

About the Author

CARLY SPADE is an adult romance writer who has been writing since she could pick up a pencil. After the insanity of obtaining a bachelor's and master's degree in cybersecurity, creating worlds to escape to still ate at her very soul. She started writing FanFiction (which can still be found if you scour the internet), and soon felt the need to get her original ideas on paper. And so the adventure began.

She lives in Colorado with her husband and two fur babies, and revels in an enemies to lovers trope with a slow burn.

Find her online:

WWW.CARLYSPADE.COM